FIRE
NIGHT

FIRE
NIGHT

PENELOPE DOUGLAS

Proofreading & Interior Formatting by Elaine York, Allusion Publishing, www.allusionpublishing.com

Also by Penelope Douglas...

Playlist

Stream the *Fire Night* playlist here
(https://open.spotify.com/playlist/
2Z9n68jD6pjIIwGkwfTXwI)

"Devil's Playground" by The Rigs
"In Noctem" by Nicholas Hooper
"Into the Night" by Julee Cruise
"Overture (The Phantom of the Opera)"
by Andrew Lloyd Webber
"Seven Devils" by Florence + The Machine

AUTHOR'S NOTE

Fire Night is a bonus novella to the Devil's Night series. It takes place about ten months **prior** to the epilogue of *Nightfall*. All of the books are entwined, and it is recommended to read the prior installments before starting this short story. If you choose to skip *Corrupt, Hideaway, Kill Switch, Conclave,* or *Nightfall*, please be aware you may miss plot points and important elements of the back story.

The entire series is available in Kindle Unlimited.

Also, if you enjoy Pinterest mood boards, all of my books come with one. Please enjoy *Fire Night*'s storyboard (https://www.pinterest.com/penelopedouglas/fire-night-2020/)   as you read!

Happy Reading!
xx Pen

To download or view the Devil's Night Series family tree, visit https://pendouglas.com/wp-content/uploads/2020/08/Family-Tree2636-scaled.jpg.

To download or view the Map of Thunder Bay, visit https://pendouglas.com/wp-content/uploads/2020/07/Map-scaled.jpg.

"THERE ARE CHORDS IN THE HEARTS
OF THE MOST RECKLESS WHICH CANNOT
BE TOUCHED WITHOUT EMOTION."
-EDGAR ALLAN POE,
"THE MASQUE OF THE RED DEATH"

FOR Z. KING

Kai

I always loved my parents' house. I was the only one out of my friends who didn't mind being home.

Michael's home life had bored and aggravated him, and Damon wanted to be wherever we were. Will had it pretty good growing up, but he'd needed action. If trouble didn't find him, he'd go looking for it.

I'd wanted to be home, though, and years later, there was still a comfort in walking through the front door of the house I grew up in.

"Ah!" A distant roar boomed as I stepped inside.

I smiled as I closed the door behind me, recognizing Banks's growl. She was in my father's dojo, either winning or *really* losing.

Inhaling, I drew in the clean scent of fresh air and leaves, the whole house permeated by the smell of the herbs and plants my mother grew in the solarium off the kitchen.

I reached out, brushing the philodendron tree and bamboo palm as I walked down the hallway.

While the exterior of the house blended with the English country estate-style of the other homes in the neighborhood,

1

the inside was very different. The uncluttered, clean, minimalist design suited my father's taste. Natural elements like plants, stones, and sunlight brought the outside in, which helped during the long winter months indoors.

But whereas the Japanese-style favored white and bright, my mother's influence was evident, as well. Dark teak floors, rugs, and color splashed about here and there. It always felt like you were walking into a cozy cave. My parents were good at compromise, and I always felt safe here.

Candles glowed inside their sconces on the wall, ready for Fire Night. Christmas wasn't for a few days, and while my parents didn't really rush to indulge the new yule tradition in Thunder Bay, they knew Jett and Mads loved it, so they obliged.

I brought my hands up, blowing warm air against my chilled fingers, feeling my icy wedding band.

"Grandma..." I heard Jett giggle.

Peering around the corner, I leaned against the door frame and watched my mom turn away and laugh as my daughter threw a pinch of flour at her, her own nose and cheeks dusted with powder, too.

I dropped my eyes, seeing my daughter's bare feet sticking out behind her as she knelt on a stool and continued kneading the dough. Eight years ago, I could fit those things in my mouth. She was growing too fast, and I kind of wanted time to stop.

Or I wanted more kids.

That was until I went over to Damon's house and then I'd be running out the front door ten minutes later with a migraine. Their nanny day drank, and I wasn't even going to pretend that I didn't understand why.

I watched my mom and my daughter working side by side, just happy they were happy. Mads had come along with his mom and sister, but he was nowhere to be seen at the moment. Probably tucked away in the wine cellar, reading. He had a nook to hide in at every house. A corner deep in the garden maze at home. A closet at Damon's. The gallery at St. Killian's. A window seat behind the drapes at Will's.

While I worried about him in ways I didn't worry about Jett, I always knew where to find him. He never scared me.

"I gotta go to the bathroom," Jett announced, hopping off the stool.

"Wash your hands," my mom told her.

Jett scampered to the mud room, wiping her flour-coated hands on her little apron, and closed the door.

I stepped into the kitchen. "You're a good mom, you know?"

My mom glanced at me, pausing with her hands in the bowl.

"You should have had a house full of kids," I told her.

She smiled to herself, working the dough as I came up behind her and wrapped my arms around her shoulders. I tucked my chin into her neck playfully.

"You were enough," she said.

"Maybe too much?"

"Oh, yeah." She scoffed. "Way too much."

I chuckled, appreciating the jest even though she wasn't really lying. Getting arrested and imprisoned was hell for them, and I was ashamed enough for the disappointment and heartache I'd caused, but even more so since I was their only child. I hated myself for not doing better.

I glanced down at the small silver pendant hiding behind my mother's apron. St. Felicitas of Rome. I squeezed her tighter, and she paused, letting me.

She loved being a grandmother.

"They still in the dojo?" I asked, pulling back and plucking one of the slices of a mandarin orange from the little bowl that was probably Jett's snack.

I stuck it into my mouth.

"For two hours now," my mother replied. "Go see if she's still alive."

"My wife can take that old man."

I walked toward the hall, feeling my mother's eyes on me. I stopped and threw a look over my shoulder, shaking my head. "Never mind. I knew that was stupid when I said it."

She laughed, both of us knowing we still hadn't seen one person who could take my father.

"You're coming tonight, right?" I asked her.

I saw her chest fall in a heavy sigh and her hooded eyes shoot me a look. "I feel like a calm evening, thank you."

"What do you mean? It'll be calm."

Her eyebrow arched up, and I bit back my laugh.

Okay, okay.

"Maybe," she said, returning to her work.

I shook my head and turned, smiling. *It had better be fucking calm tonight.*

I headed down the hallway, exited the sliding door, and stepped into the rock garden. The miniature trees, bushes, and ponds covered with snow created a peaceful oasis in the open air at the center of the house. Banks and I had created something like it at our home in Meridian City, which was a feat, considering she preferred the wild overgrowth and garden maze of our house here. I favored the more stylized landscape that I grew up with.

Clouds hung low, promising more snow tonight, and I could smell the ice in the air. Devil's Night was in our blood, but Fire Night was starting to become my favorite. I loved this time of year.

Coming to the door, I slid open the panel and spotted them immediately, sparring in the center of the dojo as I quietly slipped inside and closed the fusuma behind me.

4

Festivities in town had already begun, and we were going to be late, but my heart swelled, and I couldn't interrupt just yet. I loved watching Banks and my father. I loved watching her spend time with my parents.

"You're looking at me," my father said, blocking her kick.

She charged him, hair that had come loose from her ponytail hanging in her eyes, and sweat covering my dad's chest and neck.

He blocked a punch, advancing on her. "Stop looking at me," he barked.

She retreated when she should've circled him to gain time.

"When you watch me, you don't see," he told her. "You must see everything."

She growled, throwing a punch and then a high kick, the latter he caught and threw off without so much as a scowl of those severe black eyebrows of his. Mads looked more and more like him every day.

I folded my arms over my chest, remaining in the shadow of the beam that stretched to the ceiling as I watched my wife stumble to the side, breathing hard and already worn out.

We trained at Sensou several times a week. She was in great shape. Or should've been.

My father approached her, dressed in loose black pants with more sweat matting the salt and pepper hair to his forehead.

He pulled her back up and stared down at her. "Close your eyes."

Her back was to me, but she must not have listened, because he said it again.

"Close your eyes," he urged.

She stood there, and after a moment, I noticed her shoulders square and her breathing even out.

"In," he said, inhaling with her. "Out."

A smile pulled at my lips as a few snowflakes fluttered to the still ground outside the windows.

I remembered this lesson.

"Again," he said.

They both inhaled and exhaled slowly as he waited for Banks's mind to clear.

"Keep your eyes closed," he instructed.

Her arms hung at her side, and she continued her steady breathing.

"Do you see me?" he asked. "Do you still have the picture of me in front of you in your head?"

"Yes," I heard her reply.

"What do you see?"

She hesitated.

"What do you see exactly?" he clarified.

"Your eyes."

"And?"

"Your face."

He studied her for a moment and then continued. "Zoom out. Now what do you see?"

"The...the room around you?" she answered.

He inched in, calming his voice. "Breathe," he whispered. "What else do you see? Make me move."

She cocked her head a little, like she was watching a scene in her head. "Your arms and legs."

"And?"

"Your feet," she said. "They shift."

Finally, he nodded as if she'd finally seen what he wanted her to see. "If you look too closely, you won't see anything. Do you understand?"

She nodded.

She needed to see but not specifically, as if everything in her vision, even the peripheral, was the focus. I saw them, but I also saw Frost, my mother's cat breathing quietly on the rafter above. I could see Banks and my father facing each other, but also the snowflakes almost floating in the air outside.

"Open your eyes," he instructed.

He took a step back and fell into a fighting stance. "Zoom out."

Before she could move into position, he stepped and threw a fist. She shot her hand up and knocked it away, and then quickly dodged another fist as it came in.

I smiled.

And then, they were at it. She jumped into a stance, and in less than a moment, fists and feet flew everywhere. Arms and legs swept, flying, and grunts filled the room as he caught her thigh and she landed a fist in his side.

They moved, Banks advancing on him and then him on her, their steps flitting across the mat as they circled each other. One hand knocked away a fist before the other came in and pushed away another.

I couldn't follow what each of them were even doing, they were moving so fast. Arm up, wrist hitting wrist, and then the kicks flying through the air only to be defended.

It was like a dance.

My heart pounded as I watched a smile cross my father's face, my breath stopping for a moment, and then...

He stumbled back a couple of steps, she came in with another punch, and he caught her wrists just in time, stopping her.

He smiled, Banks frozen, as hard breaths filled the room and she stared at my dad.

Jesus. He'd stopped first. She'd worn him out.

I covered my smile with my hand, pride swelling my heart. Soon, Mads and Jett would be just like that, and while I'd never anticipated danger in our future, I knew it was possible. I breathed easier, knowing my family was at least a little prepared for anything that might come.

But not tonight. Tonight was for partying.

Releasing her, he straightened and walked up to her, taking her shoulders. They hadn't acknowledged my presence, but my father probably knew I was here.

Her body moved up and down as she tried to catch her breath.

He gazed down. "Good," he said in a gentle voice.

She stared up at him, but then I saw her head drop and her jaw flex.

"Now go have fun tonight," he told her.

I pushed myself off the wall and walked over to Banks as she turned and met my eyes. Tears hung in hers, and she quickly looked away as my father headed out the way I came in, nodding as he passed me.

Tipping her chin up, I looked down at her beautiful face, glowing with a light layer of sweat and her green eyes glistening.

She glanced after my father, Jett passing him in the rock garden and giving her grandfather a salute as he passed. He returned the gesture.

"You're very lucky, you know?" Banks said, her voice shaking. "He's proud of you."

I touched her face.

"You're so lucky," she said again, and I could hear the crack in her voice.

Bringing her in, I kissed her forehead as she shook with more tears.

"He's proud of you, too," I whispered.

Taking her in my arms, I held her tightly, hating all the memories she didn't have. How she'd suffered without parents, and how much I'd taken for granted. My father was never particularly warm, but he was far from Evans Crist or

Gabriel fucking Torrance. He was a good man, and she was more than thirty years old before she got to know what a real father felt like.

"He's so proud of you, baby," I told her again.

Warm or not, my father was never not here for any of us. We were all lucky.

Jett approached, her arms wrapping around us—as far as she could reach anyway—and joined in on the hug. I chuckled, holding my girls.

After a moment, Banks dried her eyes and drew in a deep breath, pulling back a little.

She looked down at our daughter. "Help me with my makeup?" she asked.

But I stopped them right there, telling Jett instead, "Actually, go ask Grandma how to repot a chestnut," I said. "I need to help Mommy with her shower first."

"Kai..." Banks chided.

What? I gaped at her. *What were grandparents for anyway?*

• • •

"Aren't you cold?" Banks slipped her arms around mine, hugging me for warmth.

I inhaled the crisp, evening air and blew out the steam, taking in the snow hanging on the evergreens and the bare, black branches of the maples stretching up into the night sky.

"I love it," I told her, listening as we stood outside my parents' house an hour later. "Everything is so quiet."

I looked down at her, admiring how it barely took her any time at all to get dressed. Her red strapless gown glittered, stunning with her dark hair curled and pinned to the side at the nape of her neck. She was gorgeous.

She and Jett had both decorated their faces, looking like cute clowns with white diamond shapes over their eyes and jewels glued to the points.

I threw the black cloak around her and tied it as she dug into the inside pocket and pulled on her gloves.

"The cold slows the spread of molecules," I explained. "Less pollution. The air is so clean."

And quiet. I loved winter the most for that reason. The stars peeked out through the clouds, and you could hear water in the distance, although there was no water nearby. The frozen blanket over the land in the stark night silenced the world so much, you could hear things you normally couldn't.

It was haunting.

"Snow's coming," she told me. "We better hurry."

Yeah. "Just enjoying the calm before the storm," I teased.

And I didn't mean the snow. My mother was right. Drama always went down when the family got together.

Mads walked out of the house, straightening his black tie over his black shirt and suit, and Jett came running past him and up to me.

I scooped her into my arms, her pink dress and white tights picked out by her mom who never wore pink in her life. Ever.

She smiled at me, her white teeth peeking out at me through red lips. "Fire Night is my favorite," Jett said, looking up at the flickering lanterns lining the driveway.

"You ready to go light some more candles?" I asked.

She nodded. "Can we walk?"

I opened my mouth to tell her no, knowing this wasn't a quick jaunt, especially with Banks in a long gown and high heels, but...

Her mom tightened her cloak around her and chirped, "Absolutely."

10

I set Jett down and took her hand, she and Mads walking between Banks and me as we set off.

My parents' house was on the opposite side of town from St. Killian's, and even though the trek would be cold, I wouldn't complain about getting to enjoy the evening a while longer. I just hoped Banks didn't sprain an ankle on the way.

The moon glowed overhead as we crossed the street and strolled through the park, more lanterns carving our path with their firelight.

That was the rule tonight. No electric lights.

Not that it was a law or anything we enforced, but everything looked different in the firelight, and I wasn't sure which one of us set the standard, but everyone seemed to agree it was beautiful.

In no time at all, it was tradition. Once the sun set on the winter solstice, Thunder Bay was lit almost entirely by fire—candles, lanterns, bonfires...

Voices carried on the breeze, the choir at the cathedral singing in the distance and warming the frost in the air and the slumbering roots under our feet.

Gazing left, I saw the fires in the village, much of the town enjoying the festivities and the parade, and slowly, I turned my head, seeing all the flickering flames dotting the town.

Nothing, not even Devil's Night, was more magical, because tonight was the longest night of the year. It was special.

Snow started falling around us more heavily, and Mads and Jett led the way across the bridge, flakes dotting their black hair.

"Look!" Jett pointed over the edge, out to the river flowing below.

A small tugboat puttered toward us, white lights decorating its exterior, and we all stood there as the kids watched it disappear under the bridge, and then they raced to the other side to see it coming out.

Banks and I stayed, gazing toward the village, beyond which were Cold Point, Deadlow Island, and our resort, Coldfire Inn. The music, the lights, the town dressed in snow... I inhaled long and deep, tightening my arms around her and content to stay in this spot all night.

"I love our life," she whispered, staring out at the river.

Pressing my lips to her temple, I closed my eyes, feeling it too.

Absolute contentment during these rare moments of calm.

But I sighed, knowing it would take her brother point three seconds to fuck that up tonight.

Michael and Will might take a little longer.

We headed off, crossing the bridge and hiking across the quiet lane over to St. Killian's, bowls of fire dancing down the long driveway, and torches posted on the house around the perimeter.

Jett's eyes lit up with excitement.

Rika did it for the kids, but the whole idea behind Fire Night had been Winter's.

"There's the boys!" Jett yelled, the snow falling a little heavier.

I nodded, seeing Damon's kids running around under the canopy of trees off to the side, playing hide-and-seek in the dark.

"Go play," I told her.

She ran off, hiding behind a trunk, her shiny, black Mary Janes kicking up snow as steam billowed out of her mouth, giving away her position.

Mads climbed the steps and immediately veered up the stairs, his favorite hiding place off to the left.

Banks pressed herself into me, touching her lips to mine and holding it for several seconds. "I need to talk to Em and Rika, okay?"

I nodded, letting her go.

She climbed the spiral staircase, the railing dressed with evergreens and ribbons, and I looked up after her, watching her disappear into the dark gallery above. Then, I reached over and snapped the bud of a rose from the bouquet on the small table and fitted it into my lapel.

No guests had arrived yet, the candelabras still dark and the tree unlit. The kids laughed and screamed outside as the snow fluttered down from the sky, and I walked toward the window to watch them play before all the events of the night began.

But then I heard something above me and looked up, going wide-eyed as I spotted Octavia dangling off the railing overlooking the second floor above.

"Tavi!" I burst out.

Sword in one hand, she hung with the other, her little face etched with anger.

But then she slipped and dropped, and I gasped, shooting out and catching her in my arms. "Oh, shit. What the hell?"

I cradled her, my heart in my fucking throat as I tightened my hold around her small body, my nails digging into her black embroidered pirate coat and leather boots.

I looked down, meeting her scowl. "You okay?"

"I'll slit your throat, you dog!" And she pressed the plastic blade of her toy sword into my neck.

Oh, Jesus. I rolled my eyes.

I swung her up and tossed her over my shoulder, walking toward the kitchen.

"And you're definitely your father's daughter," I teased.

Zero sense of what could've just happened to her. And zero care.

"Let me go!"

"Not a chance," I retorted. "What were you thinking, huh?"

"I was sneaking up on the vermin!" she explained, trying to squirm and kick out of my hold. "He's trying to poach me crew!"

I entered the kitchen, sidestepping the caterers, and plopped Octavia down on a side counter, out of the way.

"You need to be careful." I looked down into her black eyes. "Do you understand?"

She dug in her eyebrows, accentuating the little scar she had over the right eye from a tumble she took when she was two.

"Your parents wouldn't be happy if you cracked your little skull open." I walked over to the fridge and plucked out a juice box, slipping the straw in for her. "Your dad wouldn't be able to take it. You know how much everyone loves you?"

"I'm not afraid of anything."

I stopped and stared at her. That kind of talk could lead down a dark path I knew well.

I walked over, and instead of giving her the juice, I set it down on the counter and planted my palms on either side of her. "Look at me," I told her. "I know you're not afraid. But fear and caution are two different things. If anything ever happened to you, your dad wouldn't survive it. Do you understand that?"

Barely five years old, she stared at me with a blank look on her face.

"A true captain leads by example." I tapped her head with my finger. "A true captain uses her head, okay? Someday you're going to learn that your life can change in a moment. Caution is smart, and smart people find a better way."

"But how do you learn the difference between fear and caution?" a voice asked.

I stood upright again and turned, seeing Damon lingering in the doorway. He was partially dressed for tonight—black pants and shined shoes, his hair in place. But he was still missing his jacket and tie, and his white shirt had the sleeves rolled up.

"By experience," he answered when I didn't.

He walked over, and my spine steeled, because our parenting styles had become just another area in which we strongly disagreed. With anyone outside our family I wouldn't care, but when my kids were used to more discipline, it was getting harder and harder to explain why his were allowed to swing from the rafters.

"And by guidance from people who know more," I countered as he scooped up his daughter into his arms.

He looked at Octavia, cocking an eyebrow. "People who've surrendered to the rules and lost their imagination, he means."

I hooded my eyes. "Does Daddy let you cross streets by yourself?" I asked her.

She sucked on her juice, knowing even at this young age not to involve herself in our dumb spats.

"Because, like I said..." I smiled bitterly at Damon. "'Guidance from people who know more.'"

"And how do you determine those who are worth listening to?" he asked Octavia, but he was really just trying to piss me off. "You don't. You listen to yourself."

"And while you're doing that," I told her, "don't forget to remind yourself that choices have consequences you'll have to live with for the rest of your life. You'll make better choices with guidance."

"Did you?" Damon finally looked at me, our stint in prison not needing a reminder for me to understand what he meant.

Prick.

He came from a bad home. I came from a good one. We both still went to prison.

God, I hated him.

I mean, I'd definitely jump off a bridge for him, but...

He took his daughter and his self-satisfied smirk and walked out, and I fought the urge to throw something at the back of his head.

I just saved his kid's life. Or, at least a few broken bones.

But hey...*it would've been experience for her. Put some hair on her chest. Rawr.*

I stalked out of the kitchen, the sugary vanilla scent of cookies, macarons, and other sweets filling the house as servers carried trays to the dining room.

Madden had joined Ivar in lighting the candelabras, each making their rounds around the house, and I headed into the ballroom but stopped, seeing Damon again.

The lights had been extinguished, the candles glowing across the gold and red floor as holiday garlands of evergreens, mistletoe, and sugar plums draped across the mantel to the right, matching the ones wrapped around the railing of the staircase behind me.

The dance floor was still nearly empty, except for my wife dancing with her brother.

Hanging back, I folded my arms over my chest, softening at the sight of them together. *Okay, okay.* I didn't hate him. I couldn't hate anyone who loved her.

He dipped her back and twirled with her, and she smiled so wide before laughing and throwing her arms around him as he went faster and faster.

I smiled, watching them.

Nearby, Rika danced with Jett, both of them watching their feet as Rika counted, helping Jett with the steps. Her black gown stretched with the small baby bump, now about five months along.

Will's daughters, Indie and Finn, twirled around the couples, pretending they were ballet dancers, the black feathers in Finn's hair making my stomach sink a little at the memory. Seemed like yesterday Banks and I were in the ballroom of the Pope, watching Damon's mother, dressed in her black feathers, move around the floor like a ghost. A chill ran up my spine.

"Kai?" someone said.

I looked behind me, seeing Winter descend the stairs, holding the railing with both hands.

I reached for her, guiding her to me. "Yep, here," I said. "Did you smell me?"

How else would she have known it was me?

She laughed, joining me at my side. "Mm-hmm. You smell goooood."

I smiled, turning my eyes back to the ballroom. My son had disappeared, and Ivarsen had joined his brothers, running past us toward the dining room and the sweets, no doubt.

Headlights approached outside, guests starting to arrive.

"Octavia doesn't want to go to the lock-in tonight," Winter told me.

"Then Mads won't go, either."

"Nope."

Which was why she was telling me, so I was prepared. As the adults danced the night away or took part in the revelry of the festivities, the kids would go have their own adventure at the theater. Until midnight, anyway, when they could come home and open presents.

Winter had done a beautiful job, making this time of year special. She loved Christmas but always felt the day was bittersweet, because it meant the season was pretty much over. We started our festivities on the solstice now, happy to enjoy that we had days of joy still ahead of us.

"She's a very lucky kid," Winter said. "Lots of people who dote on her."

I nodded, seeing a shadow on the second floor. Mads had retreated to his hideaway again.

"She's an adventurer," I replied. "Mads isn't. He can live vicariously through her."

"And she loves that she can drag him anywhere," she added, "and he never gets upset with her. Her brothers are... not so flexible."

Her brothers were trouble. At least Mads set a good example.

The speakers turned off as the orchestra finished tuning, silence filling the air throughout the house.

"I love that sound," Winter whispered.

"What sound?"

"The draft of this old place hitting the flames," she said. "Do you hear it?"

I trained my ears, the wind howling through the floors above us, their gusts making the flames flicker.

The hair on the back of my neck rose.

"Feels like ghosts," she murmured. "Everything is more beautiful in the firelight, isn't it?"

I looked down at her, her long lashes draping over eyes that could no longer see anything beautiful, but that didn't mean anything was lost on her, either. She just saw it differently now.

Turning, I took her hand in mine and her waist in my other, and guided her onto the dance floor. "Hold on."

Her lips spread into a big smile, and we glided, me leading her to no music as tendrils of hair fell into her face. Her black gown fanned out behind her, and the red ribbons in her hair fluttered.

"You're pretty good," she told me.

"Shocked?"

"Well..." She shrugged, not elaborating.

We spun and moved, faster and faster until she was giggling, but she never lost her footing, lighter than air in my arms.

I guess she thought I only excelled at combat, but my mother raised a gentleman, too.

"Never give a sword to a man who can't dance," I recited Confucius as we slowed down.

She pinched her eyebrows together, breathing hard. "Why?"

"Because a weapon of death shouldn't be in the hand of someone who hasn't lived."

You can't speak for a world when you only understand one point of view.

I stopped and stared at her, an idea forming. "I want you to teach Mads and Jett how to dance."

She cocked her head.

Why hadn't I thought of it years ago? I assumed getting a good education and learning to defend themselves would make them strong, but I still had time to encourage what made them happy. Mads would hate dancing, but someday, he might value the knowledge.

After a moment, she nodded. "Okay."

Just then, Damon cut in, taking his wife's hand and waist in his own. "Excuse me."

I backed off, letting him in, and was about to go grab my own wife when I saw her heading toward me already.

"Guests are arriving," she said. "Let's go light the chandelier."

Oh, that's right.

"Jett," I called, waving my daughter toward me. "Indie? Finn?"

Guests began drifting in, Rika and Michael standing near the door to greet people as coat checkers took the ladies' wraps and gloves. Emory, dressed in green and her hair pulled into a low ponytail and curls falling down her back, circled the chandelier, handing out markers and bay leaves to all the kids.

Spreading out on the foyer floor, guests moved around them to watch as the kids wrote their wishes for the new year ahead on the leaves in silver marker and then stood up, lighting them on fire with a candle from the chandelier.

"Why do we burn it?" Gunnar asked as Dag dropped his ashen leaf into the copper bowl Emmy held.

"It releases the wish into the universe," Indie explained.

"Well, I wished for fame last year," her sister retorted, "and it didn't come true. I think we're doing this wrong."

I smiled, watching all the kids, one by one, rise up and toss their burning leaves into the dish.

"It hasn't come true *yet*," Winter chimed in.

Will started the ritual about eight years ago. A new tradition. A way to keep ceremony in our lives and something fun for the kids to remember and maybe pass on to their own children someday.

My gaze stopped at Mads, seeing him hold his leaf to the flame, but instead of lighting it, he pulled it back. Tucking it inside his suit jacket, he turned to help Octavia, steadying her hand as she touched the leaf to the flame.

A figure appeared on the stairs, and I looked up, seeing Athos descend in an extremely form-fitting silver gown with a low-cut V neckline that I'd have a hard time seeing my daughter wear when she was seventeen.

Her face glittered with gray and white makeup around her eyes, and her hair hung down her back with a pair of small antlers secured on her head, making her look like something from *A Midsummer Night's Dream*.

20

Alex had taught her how to do her makeup when she was ten, but unfortunately, Alex wasn't here to suffer Michael's wrath tonight. She and Aydin were spending the holidays with his family in New York, and we were also missing Micah and Rory, who were in Fiji.

Misha and Ryen were invited, but I doubted they'd show.

Michael walked over, turning to keep his eyes on her as she passed. "You're wearing that to the lock-in?"

"To the ball."

"We've had this conversation," he argued as she kept walking. "Twenty-one and over, Athos."

"Luckily, my daddy owns the place," she threw back.

I snorted, watching her disappear into the ballroom.

Michael rubbed his face with his hand. "I don't even know why I try." He sighed and turned around. "I need to pick less fights, because the more I lose, the more emboldened she gets."

"You can say no, you know?"

But he just shot me a look like I was crazy. "I didn't raise that kid to take no for an answer."

Oh, right.

He smiled over at me, mischief behind his gaze. "So, did you give it to her yet?"

I cocked an eyebrow. "Not yet," I muttered, not wanting Banks to hear. "Can I count on you for a calm night tonight, so I can enjoy my wife?"

"Why are you asking me?"

"Because every holiday, shit hits the fan over something," I barked.

He thinned his eyes. "Thanksgiving was not my fault."

"The Fourth of July was your fault."

He folded his arms over his chest as the kids finished lighting the candles. "And who gave Thunder Bay's basketball team your uncle's trucks last March so they could dump manure all over Falcon's Well after losing the state championships?"

"Not me," I shot back, digging out invisible dirt from underneath my fingernail. "I simply left the keys out. I didn't *give* them to anybody."

He scoffed, the guests filling the room around us.

"Besides, we didn't lose," I told him. "They fouled. The ref just didn't see it."

"Well, the next time you 'leave the keys out'," he said, getting in my face and lowering his voice. "Remember, my wife was on the phone with their mayor, getting screamed at for twenty-five minutes."

I opened my mouth to defend myself, but nothing came out. *Yeah, okay.* He had a point. That wasn't exactly fair, I guess.

"Fine," I said.

I'd behave tonight, but I expected the same from them. No drama.

The townspeople filled the house, some in masks and others in face paint, dresses and jewelry glittering in the candle light. I did a double-take, zoning in on their eyes to see who I could recognize in their disguises.

Some. But not all.

Something nipped at me. *This was no longer smart.* People were just walking into the house. No one was even checking invitations.

There was no security other than Lev, David, and a few others circulating the grounds, and there were no guards at the door.

We didn't invite trouble, but as the years passed, we acquired more. More land, more real estate, more power, more money... And when you get anything worth having, someone would eventually try to take it.

We'd been lucky so far. *Too lucky.*

"We ready?" Em called out.

But before I could turn back and reply, a voice boomed from the stairs. "'Lot 666, then!'"

Emmy startled, twisting around, and all of our eyes followed to see a man in a cape and a white mask covering half of his face.

"'A chandelier in pieces!'"

I laughed, putting my worries aside and recognizing Will instantly. Michael shook his head, unable to hide his smile.

The kids giggled as Will jogged down the stairs, whipping his cape all about. "'Some of you may recall the strange affair of *The Phantom of the Opera*.'"

"Daddy!" II laughed.

Will spun in a circle, making eye contact with all the kids. "'A mystery never fully explained!'"

And then, on cue, the orchestra and refurbished organ above us belted out the dramatic overture from *The Phantom of the Opera*, making the hair on my arms rise again.

The floor vibrated under my shoes, and my pulse quickened.

Winter couldn't smile any bigger if she tried.

Someone must've flipped the switch, because the chandelier began to slowly rise, climbing higher and higher toward the ceiling as we tipped our heads back to watch.

The flames on the candles flickered with the movement, and the kids started running, twirling, and skipping away into the ballroom.

I followed them in, the guests filtering in behind me, some starting to join Michael and Rika on the dance floor, while others plucked glasses of champagne off the trays of servers passing by.

Emmy carried the bowl of bay ashes, setting it on the mantel next to the menorah before walking toward me, her face still lit up.

She loved lighting the chandelier.

"Your favorite part..." I mused as she settled at my side, watching the room.

"Always," she said, gazing up the ceiling at the four small, electric fixtures above, not presently being used. "I almost wish they were all lit by candlelight."

"Too much work," I told her.

"Affirmative."

"The Bell Tower is gorgeous." I looked down at her. "I love what you've done with it. Or refused to do with it, I should say."

She shrugged. "There's beauty in the history. I don't want that erased."

I found Banks on the dance floor, she and Rika with their heads together over something.

"It's where I kissed her for the first time," I said, letting my eyes trail over my wife's bare shoulders.

"I didn't know that."

"Devil's Night." The memory played in my head. "My senior year."

The overture ended and the sound system kicked in, playing a soft, haunting tune with lyrics.

Then, Emmy said, "She was in the confessional with you that morning, wasn't she?"

I tipped my gaze back down to her. "How did you know that?"

She grinned, as if just remembering. "I was there that day. I ran into her."

"You go to church?" I teased.

But she just looked away, a coy smile on her lips. "I had my reasons."

Or secrets? Whatever. None of my business.

"The confessional," I mused. "That was the first time I talked to her, too. That day changed my life."

"Mine, too."

"If only I'd fought more for what I wanted." That day ended far worse than it had begun. "We wouldn't have missed out on years of being together."

"Me too," she added in a whisper.

Banks stole glances at me every once in a while, her red lips wet and her eyes dark. Heat covered my body as images filled my head of exactly what she'd look like wearing only that face makeup.

"I need to dance with her," I told Em and started to move onto the floor.

But then a young brunette was in front of me, her shoulders bare in a white gown.

"Kai," she chirped.

I halted, seeing my student looking a lot different than she did in her Aikido class on Tuesdays and Thursdays. "Soraya," I said, "You look great." I took her hand and leaned in, pressing my cheek to her temple for a quick embrace. "Are your parents here?"

"No." She smiled up at me. "But they are curled up in front of a fire tonight."

"Good to hear."

I tried to step around her and say goodbye, but she started talking again. "Thank you for the one-on-ones last week," she told me. "They really helped."

She looked up at me with adoring blue eyes, her silky-looking red hair hanging around her. I could almost feel Emmy's loaded smirk next to me.

Please. The kid was a...kid.

"Of course," I told her. "Practicing some of the language over break?"

"Yeah." She clutched her dress, and I looked down, watching her slowly lift the hem off the ground. "I carry it with me everywhere."

25

As the dress rose higher and higher, I saw black markings drifting up the golden skin of her leg.

"Ichi, ni, san," she recited, reading the Japanese numbers like a cheat sheet on her body.

"Yon, go, roku." She lifted the dress higher, over her knee and up her thigh. "Nana, hachi…"

Sweat cooled my forehead, and I glanced at Banks, seeing her watching us with her eyes on fire.

"Shit," I mouthed, seeing Emmy cover her smile with her hand.

"Ku." Soraya continued, the dress damn near rising up to her… "Juu," she finally said.

I swallowed, my eyes flashing back to Banks, Rika standing next to her wide-eyed and looking almost ready to laugh.

I caught sight of the guys watching me too, their lips moving, and even though I couldn't make out what they were saying, I could read their shit-eating grins.

I looked down again, trying to not see Soraya's long leg. "That's…that's good."

She dropped the dress back down. "I know the dojo is closed until after the new year, but I left my bag in the locker room." She inched closer, and I took a step back. "Will you be in this weekend? Like for paperwork or something? I can stop by. Just really quick."

Alone? While I'm in there…alone?

I darted my eyes to Banks, and at the same time, she and Rika dragged their fingers across their throats in a threat.

Emmy snorted, grabbing a glass of champagne off a passing tray. "I've seen that before. Like brother, like sisters."

Goddammit. This wasn't my fault. Banks was going to be pissy all night now.

I sidestepped the girl. "My wife will be in all day tomorrow, taking care of some things," I told her. "I'll let her know you're coming by."

And I got the hell out of there.

But as I tried to head to Banks, the guys dove in, cutting me off. "Someone's in trouble," Will teased.

"Gimme a break." The kid has a crush. Like I could control it.

I tried to search for my wife, but the dancers were spinning, and I couldn't see around the guys.

"Dammit," I muttered, sliding my hands into my pockets.

"Yeah," Michael added. "Everyone saw that."

"Shut up."

"Oh, shit." Damon laughed under his breath as he raised his glass to his lips. "Here come the gloves."

Huh? I found Banks again as Rika tried to bite back her laugh, clearly talking Banks down as my woman shot glares at the teenage girl.

"See!" I turned to Michael. "What'd I tell you? Shit always hits the fan."

"Relax," he told me. "Banks trusts you. So teen queen has a crush on her sensei master."

"His tutelage marked all around her thighs..." Damon taunted.

"And my wife has knives wrapped around hers," I whisper-yelled, aware of our guests. "Shit. Look at them." I gestured to the girls, Winter and Emory having joined them. "They're planning something."

Will and Michael chuckled, not moving an inch to stop anything.

"I'm more worried about that young girl than you," Damon mused.

I was more worried about the night I had planned going to hell. My wife trusted me, but it really pissed her off when other women still didn't care that I was married. Not that it happened often, but she saw it as a sign of the most ultimate disrespect. In that way, she and Damon were more like their father than they would ever admit.

"Get her away from my pregnant wife, please," Michael said. "She looks like a bomb."

Yeah.

I started to move away, but Jett ran up to me and jumped into my arms. I caught her just in time.

"Daddy, we're going to the theater now!" she announced.

"You got everyone?" Michael asked Miss Englestat, who came up with Dag and Fane in each hand.

"Yes, sir," she told him, breathless. "Athos is staying behind, and Mrs. Cuthbert has tabs on Madden and Octavia. Everyone else is accounted for."

Damon's boys grabbed on for a hug, but Ivarsen breezed past, his thumbs tapping away on his phone.

"Hey, be good," Damon called after him.

"At everything," the kid finished for him.

I chuckled. Tree? Meet apple.

"Happy hunting." I kissed my kid on the nose and hugged her tight. "See you at midnight."

But she started kicking. "Let me go or Indie will take my seat!"

I dropped her to the floor. "Be good."

Without another word, she raced toward the foyer, one of the nannies wrapping her coat around her.

As the kids left for the next few hours—set to join the rest of the children in town for treats and festivities at the theater—the music turned a little harder and deeper, and I searched the crowd for Banks again.

But my gaze caught on something as I looked. Someone was staring at me.

Full white mask. Black cloak. Near the fireplace. I blinked and spun around, trying to find his face again as my pulse skipped a beat.

Who—?

None of the men were wearing cloaks. Now *that* would be overdressed.

But when I searched for him again, he wasn't there. A chill crawled up my back at the way he'd just stood there, the black hollows of his eyes frozen on me.

"You better go," Damon said.

Huh?

I turned to him, seeing him gesture behind me. Following his gaze, I finally caught sight of my wife as she pulled on a white, half-mask, covering her eyes and nose, looking to me as she slowly backed away into the shadows. I flexed my jaw even as my groin swelled with heat at how taunting she was.

Don't you dare.

I started off, following her, the man in the cloak and mask forgotten.

I sidestepped the dancers, weaving in and out of the crowd, reaching her just in time to take her arm.

"Stop," I whispered in her ear.

She tensed, refusing to turn and face me.

"I wasn't going to kill her," she said in a low voice, staring at young Soraya at the edge of the room. "Just freak her out a little."

"She's a child."

"Yes." She turned her head, challenging me. "I seem to remember being that *child's* age the first time you had your hand up my shirt."

The memory of that mysterious girl in my arms in the Bell Tower washed over me again. "*Your* shirt," I pointed out.

Not hers.

She spun around, her green eyes and eye makeup piercing me through the white mask. "I mean it," she said, inching away like she was something I could never have. "You wouldn't tolerate me teaching someone who flirted with me."

"And you wouldn't let me dictate what you're allowed and not allowed to do." I stepped forward as she retreated.

I'd admit, I kind of liked her jealousy.

But then I didn't.

I didn't like that it could be coming from insecurity.

"Don't you trust it?" I asked her.

"What?"

"That this will never end."

She needed everyone to know that I was hers, when it would save her a lot of aggravation if it could just be enough to know that *I* knew I was hers.

I stalked toward her, slow step after slow step as my eyes dropped to her tits threatening to pop over the top of her dress.

And believe me, I knew I was hers.

The man in her bed every night. The father of her children. Her partner in everything I did.

"I want to give you something," I told her.

Couples swirled around us, neither of us blinking as her eyes seemed to glow in the dim light.

"Come here now," I said.

But she didn't. She just kept backing away.

My blood started to boil. We didn't have all night. There was shit I wanted to do before the kids got back. "You're pissing me off," I bit out, digging in my heels. "You know I don't like making scenes."

But I would if I had to.

She didn't give me a chance. As soon as she reached the edge of the room, she spun around, dove through the double doors, and disappeared. I bolted after her, not giving a shit at the eyes I caught flashing our way.

Coming into the next room, dark with only a couple hidden in the corner making out, I caught sight of her red dress as she disappeared around another corner. I chased her, finally seeing her scurry up the back stairwell.

Running up after her, I wound around the spiral staircase, the stones grinding under my shoe.

Just as we reached the second floor and she tried to escape up to the third, I caught her arm and whipped her around, pinning her into the wall.

"Like I wouldn't catch you," I taunted. "I don't even know why you try."

A taper flickered on the wall, and I stared down into her eyes, my lips hovering over hers.

She rocked off the wall, but I pushed her back and hiked up her dress, pressing my hand between her legs, my fingers on fire as I rubbed her softly.

Jesus Christ. She was bare. Completely bare.

She shuddered but stopped fighting, and I grinned, loving these rare, little surprises she gave me.

No panties was so unlike her.

"What were you and the girls planning down there?" I whispered over her mouth.

"N—Nothing."

I glided my hand up the inside of her thighs, feeling my dick harden. God, I couldn't wait.

"Look at me, Nik."

Slowly, her eyes rose, unable to resist me when I used her real name.

"I want to give you something," I said, my mouth dry with need. "Reach into my jacket. Take it out."

I ran my fingers over her soft skin, and then my knuckles, needing every inch of my skin to touch every inch of hers.

She reached into my breast pocket and pulled out a handkerchief, wrapped around a small object.

I stopped rubbing her, but I didn't move my hand as she unwrapped the gift.

A silver comb laid inside the cloth, the ornate design featuring three rubies gleaming up at her.

"It was my mother's," I told her. "And her mother's."

It was one of the only things my mother had left from her family. My grandmother had had to smuggle it to her after she eloped with my father.

Her eyes flew up to mine, and I hoped she understood what the heirloom meant.

"The women in my family pass it on to their daughters," I explained. "My mom wanted to give it to you herself, but she knew that..."

I couldn't force the words out, but her eyes dropped, her chin trembling. She knew what I was going to say.

Banks hadn't gotten a lot of gifts from others in life, and none from her own parents. It still made her nervous. My mom knew it might be easier coming from me.

Raising her hands, she fitted the comb into the back of her hair and wrapped her arms around me.

Her nose brushed mine. "I want to kill anyone for trying to take you away from me."

I reached my hands around her ass, feeling the strap of blades around her leg, and lifted her into my arms. "If I ever leave you, it's because I'm dead."

I sank my mouth into hers, proving the only assurance she'd ever need, and I'd do it a hundred times a day for the rest of my life if she needed.

She'd never had shit she had to worry about losing in life, and I was going to break my back to give her everything.

God, she was amazing.

I unzipped my pants, took myself out, and fit myself inside of her, thrusting up into her right there in the dark stairwell.

"Ah," she groaned, holding on for dear life. "I love you, Kai."

"I love you too," I breathed out across her mouth. "I can't stop. I don't want to ever stop."

I pumped up into her hard and fast, frenzied, as I buried my face in her neck and she hugged me.

I registered a screech or something somewhere in the distance, and then howls from downstairs.

"Kai," she moaned, riding me back. "I think I hear screaming."

Who cares? I didn't care. The whole house could be on fire right now, and I wouldn't care.

I stared into her eyes. *A truck would have to drag me off you.*

Damon

Well, *this is new.*

A black fucking horse trotted into the ballroom, a masked rider in a cape looming over us as the music halted, the dancing stopped, and everyone moved back, giving him ample room.

I grabbed Octavia, pulling her with me. "Come here."

A few screams hit the air, while others gasped and laughed at the display.

What the hell was this? I mean, I didn't pay attention to details, but I would've remembered Michael and Rika mentioning a massive mammal riding into their house as part of the festivities.

Frickin' Athos. This reeked of Edgar Allan Poe.

The rider wore a skull mask, and I boosted Tavi up into my arms, watching her watch him, her eyes bright with excitement.

The horse stopped, everyone quieting and waiting with bated breath, and the cool air he brought with him chilled my skin.

"The phantom watches from box five," he boomed, his voice echoing. "You will see him, though he be not alive."

Octavia didn't move a muscle, everyone around using their phones to film his message.

"Bring me his mask by the bonfire's light!" he shouted, spinning in a circle to reach everyone's ears. "Your treasure awaits you before the end of Fire Night."

And then, he shot off, leaving the room, the horse's hooves clacking against the marble floor. After a moment, we heard the quick gallops as he rode away into the night.

I chuckled, looking up at Octavia's face, who was still in awe. These kids were going to have a rude awakening when they got into the world and realized there was no place like Thunder Bay.

But that was okay. If I had it my way, they'd never have to find out how much the rest of the world sucked compared to home.

"Box five?" someone said. "So, the theater, then?"

People moved, chatter overtaking the room as the younger set started to leave, gathering their coats and deciphering his clues for the treasure hunt.

"Maybe plot five?" another person added. "In the cemetery? The riddle said the phantom wasn't alive, so..."

"Could it be a grave?" another woman chimed in.

"But he's 'watching'," another one argued, replaying the message on his phone. "A statue? Situated from a vantage point, maybe?"

Guests filtered out of the room, the younger ones dashing into the night to try to be the first to win the million dollars in trust they could either use for college or—since many already had college paid for—they could access it when they graduated, most of whom would use it to travel, invest, or start their own business.

About half the guests remained, the music, dancing, and conversations starting again as I set Octavia down and held her hands, swaying with her.

"Why can't I go tonight?" she asked.

"Because our family is hosting the hunt." I looked down at her as she stepped onto my shoes and let me lead. "It wouldn't be fair if we won it, right?"

"It's not fair anyway."

Are you pouting?

I stared down, amused. "On your birthday, do you get presents or give them?" When she didn't answer, I answered for her. "It's the same difference. The hunt is a present to the town from us. There are other treasures for you out there."

I looked over, seeing Christiane stumble as she tried to dance with her husband, Matthew, his pathetic demeanor as superbly fantastic as his son's dumb attitude. I mean, what was she thinking, marrying him? He barely had the courage to manage a sentence. He was quiet. She was quiet. That house must be a party every day. How did they decide when to have sex? Through text?

And then an image of them having sex invaded my brain, and I bit back the snarl before it escaped.

"Where are they?" I heard Octavia ask.

I blinked, turning back to her. "Where's what?"

"My treasures."

"You have to find them," I told her. "And fight for them. Nothing is given."

Her lips twisted to the side, and I almost laughed. I wanted her to dream, but this was where dreams were dangerous. Nothing ever happened how you wanted it to. It was going to be harder than she thought, and she would fail many times before she won. That was what she didn't know yet.

It wasn't the fight that got you. It was the lure that you could always quit.

She could use some practice.

I stopped dancing and dug into my breast pocket,

handing her the parchment I'd cooked up. "I had a feeling you'd be sulking."

She took the folded paper and opened it up, her black fingernail polish chipped as she took in my present for her.

She gasped. "A treasure map!"

I pointed up. "It's somewhere in this house. Above us."

She darted her eyes around the room, finally tipping her head back and gazing up to the railing of the dark gallery on the second floor.

"Can I have help?" she asked me.

We couldn't see anyone, but we knew who was up there, and I knew whom she was referring to.

I nodded. "Mmm, go ahead."

I'd put some words on the map she might need help reading anyway.

She started to run away, but she bumped right into someone, and I moved to catch her, but he was way ahead of me. He grabbed her shoulders and set her right again before standing up straight.

I looked up, seeing a man in a full white mask and a cloak step back, look at her, and then take a dramatic bow.

"M'lady," he said.

"Sorry," she chirped.

And then she ran away, heading for the stairs to fetch her cousin. I chuckled, nodding at the man as he passed, and thankful my kid was tough but also polite.

I looked back at him, noticing the cloak. A little overdressed, but okay.

I glanced upstairs, seeing a shadow pass the ceiling as Tavi ran for Madden.

He always hid during functions like this. Kai tried to explain he was uncomfortable in social situations, but I think it was a courtesy on Mads's part. Guests were uncomfortable when he was around.

Slipping my hands into my pockets, I drifted around the room, gazing at my wife as she danced with Kai's father, his wife deep in conversation with a few ladies from the garden club. I caught Rika's eyes as she stood near the fireplace, munching on another green tea macaron.

She froze, seeing me watch her. I cocked an eyebrow. *Another one? You want a cake, too? Maybe two cakes, Rika?* She hesitated only a moment and stuffed it into her mouth, followed by another one, before flipping me off and stalking away with her chipmunk cheeks full of unhealthy food for the baby.

I laughed, just teasing her. Winter had had her cravings, as well. *Live it up.*

I gazed back at my wife, loving her this time of year most of all. She adored the music, the food, and all the little things. She couldn't see the lights, but in a way, she did. She said they made the house feel different. Warmer, somehow.

I loved that nothing escaped her. Even the scent of wrapping paper. It had never occurred to me wrapping paper had a scent, but she made me lie down under the tree every winter and inhale the presents.

She was right. I noticed it now.

Kai and Banks walked back into the ballroom from wherever they had been hiding, Banks's hair now hanging down around her as Kai straightened his tie. Will twirled Emmy around the now-spacious dance floor, since some of the guests had left, his laughter filling the room.

But then I saw Matthew head across the room, through the center hall, into the dining room.

Christiane wasn't with him. I immediately searched for her.

Spotting her as she drifted in the opposite direction, I hesitated a moment, watching her disappear into the next room. I tensed, something nipping at me as it did more and more the past couple of years.

In the days, months, and decade since I'd found out Rika's mother was also mine, I waited for what I was sure was coming from her.

Failure.

At some point, she'd relapse. She'd forget one of my kids at the store or the park. The novelty of being a loving, attentive, and responsible grandmother would wear off or take too much energy to keep up with, and she'd slowly disappear from our lives.

No matter how cold I could be, or the years of answering her in one-word responses, nothing had fazed her, though. She was nothing, if not patient.

As time passed, the opposite happened. Instead of her giving up, my fight began to lose its steam. It was hard not to love how indulgent she was with Octavia—making almost all of her clothes by hand, since there really wasn't any quality period clothing in the style Tavi liked that didn't look like some cheap costume.

She was amazing with Gunnar, always thoughtful in scrounging yard sales for spare parts he could use for his inventions, and she didn't mind when Fane and Dag destroyed her house, building forts in every room.

She'd been a huge help when Winter was in the hospital giving birth to Octavia, one of Kai's dogs nearly bit off Ivarsen's ear and he was only six. She stayed in the hospital room with him two floors down when I had to be with Winter.

I didn't want to swallow my pride. It felt like I was fucking choking.

But more and more, I was also starting to hate the hurt in her eyes she tried to cover up when I ignored her. I didn't used to care.

Something had changed.

I followed her, my feet moving without thinking.

Pulling open the white door, I slipped into the next room, a smaller ballroom, dark and vacant. She stood at the window, the moonlight making her sparkly white gown shimmer and her blonde hair—pulled back in a bun—shine.

I stood there, pulling the door closed behind me as I watched her.

It was like she was waiting for something.

"You do that a lot." I crossed my arms over my chest. "Leave rooms full of people to be alone."

She didn't turn around, just clasped her hands in front of her.

"I do it to give you an opportunity to follow me," she said. "I figured you wouldn't speak to me with others around."

"You think you know me?"

She turned her head, meeting my eyes. "You don't know me." Her voice softened. "There are so many things I need to say. Have been waiting to say."

I didn't move. *Well, let's hear it, then. You've had years to prepare.*

Part of me was dying to hear this, if for no other reason than to open old wounds and get me angry again. Angry enough to remember why I should hate her.

She'd abandoned me. Every day, for years.

She might be a good person, but did it matter? Did I need her now?

No.

She turned her body but remained in her spot. "Do you remember the toy bear I gave to Ivarsen his first Christmas?"

I still didn't move. Or respond.

But I remembered it. It was small, about half the size of him, with a red ribbon tied around its neck. It had been wrapped in old, wrinkled brown paper with a dusty bow. I remembered thinking it looked out of place among the fancy bags and boxes of the other presents she'd bought him.

She dropped her eyes, and I started to tense.

Well, what? Did she steal it while she was high? Mean to give it to Madden? What?

"That bear was yours," she told me. "It had been yours since you were a baby."

I clenched my jaw.

I heard her swallow, but she didn't come closer. "I thought I'd find a way to get it to you—and all the other presents I bought over the Christmases and birthdays throughout the years."

I stared at her, unblinking.

"The music box I gave Octavia, the toy trucks I gave to Fane, and the remote-control boat and books I gave to Dag and Gunnar..."

My throat swelled, and I tried to force down the needles, but I couldn't.

All mine. An image of all the toys wrapped, collecting dust in her attic and waiting for a kid who would never open them flashed through my head, but I pushed it away.

So what? I had all the toys I could ever want growing up. I never went without anything money could buy. I didn't miss it.

"It's my fault." She took a step toward me. "Everything that...everything you grew up with, it's not your fault. It's not theirs, even." She shook her head. "They weren't good people. We couldn't expect them to do good things, but I was a good person once, and while I didn't know how bad it was for you, I knew it wasn't good."

I balled my fists under my arms.

She let her eyes fall again, and I saw something shimmery drop off her cheek.

"I wanted to die." Her voice was thick with tears. "I deserved to die. I was trying to die."

Every muscle in my body hardened.

"God, I wanted it all to end," she whispered, her shoulders shaking. "I had no idea how ugly the world could be until your father."

She turned blurry in my vision, because that was a good way to put it. With my father, everything was dark and hell.

"I was a child." She walked closer. "I didn't even know how to ride a bike until I was eighteen. Schraeder taught me. I was so sheltered."

Tears spilled down her face, thinking about this teenage girl, younger than Rika was when I terrorized her.

Banks, Winter, Em, Rika...I had no doubt they would survive what Christiane went through, but...they would've been hurt. Badly hurt, inside and out.

Anger twisted my gut just thinking about it.

"Rika was so alone for so long," she murmured. "Quiet, meek, always pressing her nose against the glass, trying to see into a world she was waiting to be invited into. She had no voice, because I had none to give her."

I remembered.

"The years faded in and out," she continued, "and any moment of clarity was like a knife in my brain. I couldn't take it. I couldn't stand to remember you. I was so weak."

I knew what that was like. I had the scars to prove it. She had pills. I had razor blades.

But it wasn't weakness for me. It was coping. I had to do something.

"But she eventually found her way, didn't she?" she asked, not waiting for an answer. "Michael, Kai Mori, Will Grayson... you. I should've known life would find a way to take care of her when I failed to. I should've known you'd find each other."

A gentle smile flashed across her lips. "She speaks like she has ten-thousand soldiers behind her now. You did that. Not me."

Rika learned everything she didn't want to be by seeing firsthand every day what a wasted life looks like, just like Banks and I did in my house.

"And you're happy," she told me. "Winter did that. Not me."

Christiane had finally learned what she should've taught her children—instead of them teaching her—you're one-hundred percent responsible for your own happiness.

"I'm grateful the lessons she learned didn't come at too great a cost," she said, approaching me. "And I'm forever regretful yours came at so much." Her chin trembled. "I'm sorry. God, I wish I could go back and do it all differently. I would do everything differently, even if he killed me for it."

I forced down the lump in my throat, my head aching, trying to hold back the tears.

He would've killed her. Maybe she should've fought. Should've tried. Should've gotten ready for when I was old enough to approach, or gotten some help from people my father feared, but maybe it would've still ended badly, and instead of having a sick mother, Rika and I would've ended up without one.

Enough time had been wasted.

"I will be forever sorry, but I needed you to know that I love you," she said. "Always have, and there is one more present under that tree out there that those beautiful children can't have, because it was always yours. You can open it after I leave or never at all, but I needed to give it to you."

She started to leave, always ducking out, because she didn't want to overstay her welcome, but while I was curious what she got for me when I was a kid that she left under the tree, I didn't want her to leave yet, either.

"Christiane," I said.

She stopped, and I looked over at her next to me, not sure I had the stomach for this. I didn't trust parents, and I was too old to start.

But I didn't want to hurt her anymore.

Maybe I could be her son, eventually. Maybe not.

But we could try to be something.

"How is it you don't know how to dance?" I asked.

She blinked at me. She and Matthew looked like two middle schoolers at their first Spring Fling back there. I thought she was cultured.

She shifted, looking uncertain. "I don't know a lot, I guess."

The dull hum of the music drifted through the walls, but I was able to make out the tune as I turned to her.

Holding out my hand, I waited as she stared at me, looking a little shocked.

Finally, she took hold. I pulled her in, her cool hand fitting in mine as I slipped my other around her waist. My heart skipped a beat, feeling my mother in my arms for the first time.

She gazed up at me, the lines around her eyes giving away her age, but the look in them still like a child.

"Follow my lead," I instructed.

Pushing off, I moved her around the empty room, the music barely audible as we twirled and stepped. I looked down at her, something swelling in my throat, and it hurt, but I couldn't look away, either.

I didn't need her. I'd made a beautiful family, not just my wife and children, but my friends too. I had everything.

And still, holding her in my arms, I realized something that had been missing. I realized how much I wanted to bring her in closer and hold onto something.

Sometimes I was so tired. I could ask for help, lean on the guys or vent to the women, but I wouldn't. Not ever.

I wanted to be strong for them. I never wanted Banks to see me scared again, or Rika to see me lose my shit and not be able to handle something.

I never wanted my children to see me as anything less than a man.

I wasn't sure why, but with Christiane, I didn't care if I wasn't the strongest in the room. Even well into my thirties, I had to admit, I kind of still wanted a mom.

A mom might be there for the times you were vulnerable.

Pulling her in closer, I carried her around the floor, hearing her breathe out a laugh as we spun, her feet barely touching the ground the faster I moved.

How strange it was to be a parent. For so many years, I couldn't see myself in her shoes, and even though I knew I'd do so many things differently if I'd been her, I could at least understand how hard it probably was to be desperate for your child and watch another woman raise him.

Between Christiane, Natalya, and Gabriel, they did everything wrong.

But I was still here.

Banks was still here. Rika was still here. Despite everything, we survived our parents.

Not once had Banks or Rika ever blamed theirs for anything. I had done nothing but blame Christiane for the past decade.

How easily could my own kids turn around and do the same? All this love I had for them, and they could still hate me.

I slowed my feet, a weight settling on my shoulders, and I was so tired all of a sudden.

And scared. She wanted to be more, but she failed. How did I know I wouldn't? How could I stand there and judge her, acting all high and mighty? No one knew what the future held.

Christiane looked up at me, her smile falling as we stopped, but I didn't say anything.

Slowly backing away, I left her and headed back into the ballroom, immediately searching for Winter.

The music grated on my ears, and I spotted her talking to Michael and Emmy. I walked for her.

Taking her hand, I saw her smile as she instantly recognized the feel of me and grabbed hold with both of her hands.

"Where's Octavia?" she asked.

"Treasure hunting with Mads," I mumbled, pulling her with me without a word or look to the other two. "Come on."

Without question, she held onto me as I guided her into the foyer, underneath the candlelit chandelier, and to the door to the catacombs.

I pulled open the latch, ushered her inside, and closed it behind us, immediately scooping her into my arms and stepping down the stairs.

"What's wrong?" she asked, wrapping her arms around my neck.

"I need to hold you."

"You are holding me."

"You know what I mean," I said, kissing her lips.

She didn't press further, just let me carry her into the bath and set her back on her feet. The candlelight extended into the catacombs, the jacuzzi already filled with water and steam rising off the surface.

Reaching over, I turned the knob, the spouts in the ceiling springing to life, and water poured into the small pool in a circle of about twenty different streams, almost like a fountain pouring down.

I tore off my jacket and shirt, dropping them to the floor, followed by the rest of my clothes, and then got to work on Winter. I unlaced the corset and pushed down her dress before peeling off her underthings, leaving the ribbons in her hair.

Heat coursed under my skin at the sight of her, and I pulled her into my arms, lifting her up. "Come here," I gasped over her lips.

She wrapped her legs around me, and I climbed into the huge bath, the hot water sending chills all over my body.

I sat down, taking her with me, the rain shower falling around us as I hugged her to me and buried my face in her hair.

She tensed, but I just squeezed tighter, trying to feel solid again. I hated doubt, and most of the time I kept busy enough to not let myself worry about my kids, but I didn't know what I was doing any more than the next person. I could judge the people who raised me all I wanted, but it was me who'd be judged next.

"Damon..." Winter whispered, knowing something was wrong.

"I'm not a good father." I breathed out a sigh, clutching her. "Ivarsen has no discipline. He's going to be undriven. Fane is neurotic. Everything has to be perfect. Gunnar is going to blow us up with his machines. Dag has refused to eat a vegetable since birth, and Octavia's going to wind up in a fucking asylum when she finds out real life pirates are just terrorists with grenade launchers." I gulped, hating that after thousands of years there was still no proven method of raising kids. "I don't know what to do. How the hell would I know what a good parent does and doesn't do?"

I was just as ignorant as Christiane was when she had me. Kai was right. They had a better chance at life with more guidance. I was doing everything wrong.

Winter's arms finally wrapped around me, and she pressed her lips to my temple, her breasts flush against my body.

"A good parent has happy kids," she whispered in my ear. "Our kids are so happy."

She kissed my cheek and then my lips, soft and slow. I closed my eyes, reveling in the sound of the water and the feel of her.

"They're so happy," she told me again. "And so in love with you."

A flutter hit my stomach, and I smiled a little, unable to hold it back. *They do love me, don't they?*

"And I'm so happy," she added.

I pulled back, looking at her as my thoughts started to come into focus again. It didn't happen often, but it was hard not to compare myself. Kai's kids had great manners and were fairly quiet. Athos was smart, ambitious, and determined. Will's children never fought him on anything. They did what they were told the first time he asked.

My kids...

But I stopped the thought in its tracks, remembering Ivar helping his mom make pancakes this morning.

My kids could be really sweet, actually, couldn't they?

Gunnar was so good about helping with spills, so his mom wouldn't slip. Fane helped her pick out books at the store for Dag and Octavia, describing the pictures and story, so she knew what to buy.

They were good kids. I drew in a breath and exhaled, letting the worry go for now. We were doing a good job.

"Better?" she whispered, kissing my jaw and caressing my neck.

My eyelids fluttered closed, and I nodded. "Don't stop."

She grinded against me, and I started to harden, my hand

palming her breast, but then a high-pitched sound penetrated the ceiling above our heads, and we both stopped, looking up.

"Was that a scream?" she asked.

I groaned. What now?

Will

I kissed her, her red lips soft and warm as I caressed her cold cheeks. Pulling back, I gazed down at her through the intricate silver metal mask that covered her forehead, her eyes staring up at me through the slits in the design.

Leaning in, she breathed over my mouth and slid a quick hand down my pants, grabbing me. "You think your wife suspects anything?" she teased.

I gasped as she fisted me, not caring about anything right now other than to see her butt-assed naked, except for that mask on her head.

I grinned, nibbling her bottom lip. "Who cares?" I taunted. "Nothing is keeping me off of you."

Emmy smiled, sinking her mouth into mine and pulling her hand off me, so she could wrap her arms around my neck.

"I love you so much," my wife told me. "You know that, right?"

I nodded. "But you can still work hard to prove it."

"I will." She kissed me again. "But finish dancing with me first."

We spun, the music just barely drifting up to the second-floor balcony where we danced, the cold and snow seeping through to our bones, but she was smiling so much, I wasn't about to stop whatever she wanted.

She laid her head on my chest, holding me close.

I loved it when she did that. All the time I spent thinking she didn't need me, and now I knew she did.

She didn't hold me. She held on to me.

We stared out at the forest, most of the trees bare of leaves, and the Bell Tower's lantern visible through the branches.

"Where is her grave?" Emmy asked.

I didn't have to ask who she was talking about, the eternal flame for Reverie Cross flickering in the belfry in the distance.

It was strange that she'd waited so long to ask that question, but no stranger that no one else ever had.

When I didn't answer, she asked, "Did your grandfather love her?"

I tightened my arms around her. "I've never asked him."

It was a subject of which I was eternally curious, but I could never bring it up with him. Maybe I'd be disappointed if the answers were more boring than my imagination.

Maybe I was afraid the answers would change how I loved him.

"Did he kill her?" Emmy whispered.

"I *won't* ask him."

Not ever.

"He could be the only one who knows what happened that night," she pressed.

I know. And he wouldn't live much longer to tell the story.

"No one knows where her grave is, then?" she asked again.

"Nowhere near Edward's," I told her. "That's all I know."

I snuggled her close, wanting to make the most of the time we had left before the kids came home, and discussing Reverie Cross was not what I had in mind.

"So, do you love me?" I teased.

"I'm almost positive I told you I did just thirty-nine seconds ago."

I scoffed. I liked to hear it more frequently. She knew that.

She laughed, pressing her mouth to mine. "I love you."

I moved over her lips, freezing my ass off out here, but the warm promise of her body had me hard and ready.

"I want to go somewhere," I told her.

Catacombs, pantry, spare bedroom...wherever.

"I want to dance some more," she whined.

I cocked an eyebrow. "How about you dance *for* me?"

I could live with that.

A wicked smile crossed her lips, and she bit her bottom lip. "Race you."

And before I could reply, she pulled away, hiked up her dress, and started running.

A laugh rumbled through me, watching her scurry back into the house in her high heels before I sprinted, chasing her.

Bolting through the sitting room, she squealed as I tailed her and we both ran into the hallway, toward the guest rooms.

But then she halted all of a sudden and screamed, her back going rigid.

"Will!" she cried.

My smile fell, and I darted up to her side, taking hold of her.

"Wha—?"

But then I looked down and saw a bloody pool on the wooden floor, a body lying in the hallway.

I sucked in a breath and pulled her back. "What the fuck?"

"Oh, my God." She covered her mouth with her hand.

"What's going on?" Kai called from downstairs, and I looked over the railing to see him standing in the foyer.

"Hurry!" I waved him up.

Kneeling down, I tried to make out the guy's face in the dark, but he was face down, only the left side visible.

Who...? What the hell happened?

"Baby, get the lights," I told her.

I pressed my fingers, finding his neck to check for a pulse, but I couldn't find one. Light finally illuminated the hallway as footfalls hit the stairs, everyone running up after us.

"What the hell?" Kai said, stopping next to the body. "Who is that?"

How would I know?

"Is he dead?" I heard Michael ask.

No idea. I stared down at him, a young blond man in street clothes, blood seeping out of his head. I didn't recognize him, and he wasn't dressed for the party.

"Who is that?" Rika asked.

I shook my head.

Someone raced past us as I searched his pockets for identification, but when I reached under his jacket, I felt it.

I hesitated, the pulse in my neck throbbing.

Shit.

I flipped him over, dug under his arm, and pulled out the pistol from his holster. It laid in my palm, realization starting to hit all of us at the exact same time. The only people who had weapons were Lev and David, and this wasn't either of them.

"The kids are gone!" a woman shouted.

What? I shot to my feet as everyone spun around to lock eyes with Mrs. Cuthbert.

"What kids?" I barked. "They're at the theater." And then I jerked my chin at Emmy, tossing her my phone. "Call Miss Englestat." She had the kids at the theater. "Have her do a head count."

She nodded, her hands shaking as she dialed.

"Mads and Octavia," Damon murmured, his worried eyes meeting mine. "They stayed behind."

Mads and Octavia... I darted my eyes to the nanny.

"They're not in their rooms," she cried.

And my face fell, realizing those were the kids she was talking about.

Everyone ran.

"Tavi!" Banks raced down the hall to the rooms the kids used when they were here.

"Madden!" Kai bolted down the other hallway where it forked to search the gallery where his son liked to hide.

"Madden!" more voices called as everyone fanned out.

My mouth went dry. I dipped down again, searching for the dude's pulse and not finding it. Putting my fingers under his nose, I waited to feel the warmth of his breath.

There was nothing.

More footfalls ascended the stairs, and I rose up again, piecing together the possibilities in my head.

"He's dead," I said.

"It wasn't us," I heard Lev say, and I looked up to see him and David standing at the top of the stairs, out of breath. "We didn't see anything."

"That's obvious!" Banks growled.

"The door's been opening every ten seconds with guests, Banks!" Lev yelled. "Anyone could've gotten in. I told you we needed more security."

"But you all didn't want 'armed guards and a metal detector at the front door'," David added, quoting Michael.

Michael grabbed his collar, shoving him away. "Search the house. Go!"

Damon, Banks, and Michael ran in and out of rooms, searching again. "Mads!" they called. "Octavia!"

I tucked the gun into the back of my pants and gestured to Kai. "Get his feet."

"We need the police," Emmy argued. "Don't move him."

"We're not calling anybody until we find the kids," Kai gritted out.

We weren't sure how this happened. We needed to find out before we involved the cops.

"Octavia!" Damon bellowed, and I swore I could hear his frantic breathing from here.

"Wait, the cameras..." Rika burst out.

Spinning around, she ran to her office, her computer set up to access the street cams and home security. She had a view of nearly every inch of the town.

Kai and I dumped the body in her and Michael's bedroom, closed the door, flipped over the carpet in the hallway to cover the blood, and ran after everyone else, charging into her office.

"Go back," I heard Michael tell her.

Pushing buttons and turning a knob, she rewound the footage, playing back the night's events. There weren't any cameras inside the house, but they covered the exterior and the grounds. I guessed that would change after tonight. Michael would have the company here in the morning, adding extra security.

She stopped, seeing Mads and Octavia rushing out the side door of the kitchen, running frantically as if trying to escape, but...

A car was waiting. My heart lodged in my throat. Two men jumped out, and before the kids knew what was happening, they were thrown inside and the car raced off.

"No," Damon gasped.

"What is it?" Winter cried.

He just held her close.

"Wait, wait, who is that?" Kai pointed to the blond sitting in the passenger side seat. "Zoom in!"

Rika rewound again, catching him as he got out of the car to help get the kids and paused the video, enhancing the shot.

Banks whimpered. "Ilia Oblensky."

Kai's spine straightened, and he breathed hard. Ilia was an employee of Gabriel Torrance years ago. Banks had him thrown out of the country when she inherited her father's estate.

"And who's that?" Michael squinted at the other one who'd gotten out of the SUV.

"I can't tell," Rika replied.

But I stared at the brown head I'd know anywhere, because I knew him well.

My God.

"Taylor Dinescu," I whispered.

Everyone turned to look at me, my stint in Blackchurch still rearing its ugly head.

"Jesus, fuck," Damon muttered. "How did they find each other?"

I had no idea. Maybe there was Facebook group for people who hated us. A sinking feeling hit me, because I knew. I knew it years ago. He was a loose end I'd ignored, and I shouldn't have.

But then Banks twisted around. "Kai?"

I followed her gaze, seeing Kai back out of the room, rage in his eyes.

"It's my turn," he told her. "I let you deal with him last time. Not this time."

But before I could figure out what he meant, he tore from the room, and it took no time at all before we were all racing after him.

The ball still carried on downstairs, but instead of clearing the place or making some excuse to our guests, we didn't waste another minute.

"Give me your phone," Rika told Banks.

Without question, she handed it to her as we raced down the stairs. Tears spilled down Banks's cheeks, but she didn't make a sound otherwise.

"I'm logging you into the street cameras," Rika told her, tapping away on her cell. "They turned right out of the gate about ninety seconds ago, probably headed toward town, but keep an eye on them and make sure. We'll follow."

Banks nodded, Rika handed her phone back to her, and everyone rushed through the front door, grabbing keys to cars on the way.

But I caught sight of something and stopped.

They all veered around me, emptying the foyer, but I stared at the grandfather clock, it's pendulum frozen and the minute hand paused on nine minutes past ten.

Holding up my wrist, I checked my watch, seeing it was actually twenty-three minutes past the hour.

I glanced at the clock again.

"What is it?" Emmy rushed back up to me.

"Clock stopped." I couldn't breathe. "Ten-oh-nine. That's when Reverie Cross died."

I mean, I didn't really believe that shit, but I also knew Madden was the only one who refused to light a candle on EverNight. Kind of weird.

She pulled me along, both of us running to the back doors of one of the SUVs, Kai and Banks piling into the front. Michael and Damon climbed into the other car with Winter and Rika, and Kai slipped the key in, pausing suddenly.

He tapped the digital clock, and I zoned in, seeing ten-oh-nine on the car clock, as well.

"What the hell?" Kai growled.

But he didn't stop to worry. "How far ahead of us are they?" he asked his wife.

"Just reaching the village," she told him, looking at her screen. "Hurry."

We strapped ourselves in, and I shot a worried look to Emmy next to me.

"It's not EverNight," she whispered.

"It doesn't have to be."

Reverie Cross had all year to strike, and while I knew a lit flame the next morning meant you were safe, I had never cared to think about what happened to those who didn't light a candle at all.

"Let's go!" I called.

Kai shot off, slamming the gas, and we raced down the driveway, Michael's headlights bright on our tail.

Kai charged onto the road, the tires spinning under us on the snow-covered blacktop. Kicking it into low gear, he sped down the street, past the other houses lit up with bonfires, lanterns, and holiday lights.

"Did you reach Engelstat?" I turned to Emmy, remembering what I'd asked her to do.

"Yes, the kids are safe." She nodded. "Banks sent security to the theater. They'll stay there until we come."

I nodded once. *Good.*

If anything, they were probably safer there. Tons of people, the whole place locked down...

"Where are they now?" I asked Banks.

She hesitated, studying her screen and changing vantage points. "Heading toward Old Pointe Road," she finally answered and then looked to Kai. "They wouldn't be going to the resort, right? Meridian City, maybe?"

He shook his head, turning his eyes left and right as he raced at what felt like a hundred miles an hour. "Just keep your eyes on them."

I stared out the window, clenching my jaw so hard it ached. *Taylor Dinescu.* We hadn't messed with Blackchurch for him after the last time we saw him that night at the Cove. We threw everything at him and his family, sending him to prison, because he deserved to be there. Not only for what got him sent to Blackchurch, but for my own personal reasons, too.

He'd hurt Emmy. A lot. And he fucking enjoyed doing it.

And when he finally managed to get out six years ago, I hired someone to keep an eye on him for a while—make sure he didn't get any ideas—but I knew he didn't deserve a second chance. We should've sent him away.

Or dealt with him permanently. He was the one with the money. Not Ilia. If I had just taken care of it, we wouldn't be here.

"This could've been our kids," I mumbled, tears filling my eyes.

"It is our kids," Em replied.

I looked over at her as she reached out and took my hand. I couldn't imagine what Damon was feeling right now.

I wouldn't really know the full measure of it until it was one of mine.

"What happened in that room?" Banks asked Kai. "Something went wrong if they left a dead body behind. How did we not hear or see anything?"

"We're going to find them," Kai stated. "Mads is smart."

"He would've fought," Banks told him, crying again. "They would've had to hurt him to get him in that car. Did you see on the camera if they hit him or not?"

He shook his head but didn't answer.

My eyes burned, seeing Banks so scared for the first time ever. I turned my head out of the window. This would be the end of us. If anything happened to those kids...

We had minutes. Minutes before they were gone forever.

"Look at me," Kai told her, trying to keep his eyes on the road too. "Not today."

Banks nodded but still looked about to break.

I heard a seatbelt unclick, and Emmy was suddenly in my lap, forcing my face around and my eyes on her.

I closed them, though. I'd brought this on them. What if worse happened to our kids someday? What life did I bring her into?

"Look at me." She shook me.

I opened my eyes.

"We couldn't be anyone else," she said. "This isn't your fault."

I stared up at her, all the doubt and worry I was usually good about hiding laid bare for her, because she always knew what I was thinking. She could read me as well as herself.

I didn't want to be anyone else. But I didn't want the kids to suffer the consequences for our choices, either.

I wrapped my arms around her and looked up into her eyes. "I love you," I whispered. "Thank you for my children."

If I didn't get a chance to say it again...

Her smile peeked out. "Ditto."

I held on to her, her scent and eyes reminding me of our kids and everything I loved about waking up every day.

We had a right to be here, and we didn't ask for this.

Reaching down, I fisted both sides of the slit of her dress and ripped it up her thigh, giving her legs room to move. "Let's go get these motherfuckers."

She kissed me as Kai sped into the village, but immediately slammed on the brakes.

"What the hell?" he barked.

I pulled away from Em, squinting out the front windshield to see the street crowded with people, despite the thick, white flakes pouring down. I glanced over at the theater, noting Banks's two men just inside the doors, guarding the kids.

I exhaled, looking back at the costumes and masks and

fire pits glowing bright around the village as music played and people smiled.

Santa sat up in the gazebo, a line of a dozen kids waiting to meet with him.

"The treasure hunt," I reminded him. That was why everyone was out. We couldn't have planned this kidnapping better for Taylor and Ilia. Tons of activity to get lost in.

I glanced behind me, not seeing the others. Michael must've gone the long way, knowing what the village would be like.

"Head past the cathedral," Emmy told him. "Take the lane down to Old Pointe."

He hit the horn and flashed his lights as people took their sweet time getting out of the fucking way. Slowly, the snow-covered street cleared.

"Kai, go!" Banks yelled.

He swerved, past the gazebo, Sticks, and the White Crow Tavern, jerking the wheel and skidding around the corner.

Banks whimpered, holding the safety bar above her window, and I could tell she was losing her mind. Every moment those kids weren't in our arms, the more chance we had of never finding them.

I had no idea what Taylor and Ilia were planning, but if they'd wanted them dead, they would've done it at the house. There was no way they were planning on returning them, though. It'd be suicide.

Thoughts of things so much worse invaded my head, and my stomach rolled, knowing what happened to kids all over the world. The horror that might await if we lost them tonight.

I rubbed my eyes, the sweat on my forehead coating my hand.

The headlights burned a hole in the darkness ahead, snowflakes fluttering to the ground as the gun dug into my back. I was tempted to use it.

God, I was tempted to take our family over that line tonight.

"Stop!" Banks yelled. She pointed ahead, and everyone looked, seeing taillights in the ditch off the side of the road. My heart hammered in my chest as Kai swung up behind the SUV and pulled to a stop, everyone knowing without a word that it was the same car.

What the hell happened? The kids...

We jumped out of the car, the cold nipping at our faces as we ran to the crashed, black SUV.

Relief and fear washed over me at the same time.

Taylor was collapsed with his head over the steering wheel, his window partially down, and I leapt down the ravine, grabbing hold of the door handle.

"You son of a bitch!" I yelled, reaching over the window and trying to grab him. He swayed, his face bloody, but the fucking car was crashed between two trees, and I couldn't get the door open.

"Octavia!" Emmy shouted.

Followed by Banks. "Mads!"

I darted for the rear of the car and pulled open the hatch, crawling over the backseat to the motherfucker.

"They're not here!" Banks yelled, crawling in after me.

Emmy broke the driver's side window just as I reached Taylor. He swung around, pulling out a gun, but just then, she shot her hand out, knocking the weapon to the floor, and whipped the ridge of her palm right into his neck, crushing his throat.

Heh. Did Kai teach her that? Looked familiar.

Blood matted Taylor's hair and dripped down his face. I grabbed him, gripping his jaw. "Where are they?" I bellowed. "What did you do?"

But just then, I saw it. My stomach rolled, and I winced,

averting my eyes for a moment. *Jesus fucking Christ.* What the fuck?

His goddamn eyeball hung just outside its socket, blood spilling out of the other one, as well. How did that happen?

"That...that..." he gasped, trying to get the words out. "That kid is crazy. He killed Gibbons."

Huh? "Who?" I barked.

You know what, I don't care. "Where are they?" I fisted his collar, shaking him.

And where was Ilia?

Emmy moved out of the way, letting Kai in, Mads's father grabbing hold of Taylor with me, both of us squeezing his skull.

I fitted my thumb just between his nose and eye, ready to dig in. "Now, or I take the other one!"

He closed his mouth, and I barely had time to realize what he was doing before he spit in my face.

Kai growled, grabbing him and burrowing his thumb into his eyes, threatening to blind him completely.

"Ahhhh!" he screamed.

"Where?" Kai yelled.

"The marina!" he cried. "The marina!"

I scrambled out of the car, grabbing Emmy's hand as all of us raced back up to our SUV. Lev and David pulled up, climbing out of their car, having probably tracked Banks's phone.

"The Pope," Kai told them, but then he reached across Taylor and pulled out a white mask.

It wasn't one of ours. More like a full phantom mask. Did he recognize it?

Or...

My stomach sank. *They were at the party.*

Jesus Christ.

Kai threw the mask back into the car, and then stalked to ours, yanking his door open. "The twelfth floor," he instructed.

"Yes, sir," David replied.

Good idea. We weren't turning Taylor over to anyone's care this time. We had a place to hide him. If he survived.

They ran over to collect Taylor as Banks jumped on her phone. "The marina," she told someone, probably Damon. "Kill him if you have to."

And please hurry.

I opened the back door, letting Emmy in first.

"That was a good move, baby," I told her, remembering her little hand trick on his throat. "*John Wick,* right?"

"*John Wick 2.*"

I nodded, rushing in after her. "Oh, right."

Michael

"I'll keep you posted," Rika told her mom on the phone. "Don't worry." She listened, then nodded, glancing at me. "As soon as we know something, yes."

She hung up and handed the phone to me. I tucked it into my pocket, Damon in the driver's seat in front of me and Winter wringing her hands next to him.

I heard a notification beep, and then Damon tapped the screen of his cell.

"What is it?" Rika asked.

"Banks texted," he told us. "The kids are at the marina."

"Does Banks have them?" I blurted out.

But he shook his head, punching the gas, the engine revving under us. "I don't think so."

"Damon..." Winter begged, and I could see her knees shaking.

He clasped her hand. "They won't do anything."

"They might not plan to, but I doubt that dead body upstairs was planned, either," she pointed out. "Something went wrong. They'll be more scared now."

Rika scooted forward and put her hand on Winter's arm.

"If they were going to..." I started, but thought better of saying that out loud. "They would've done it at the house. They want ransom or something."

Winter paused a moment, dropping her head. "Or they're selling them," she muttered. "Or bringing them to someone else."

Jesus. I closed my eyes, groaning. We all knew the worst-case scenarios, and none of them ended happily for us if we didn't catch up to those kids in the next ten minutes.

I hated that she let those thoughts fester, but...it kept us alert, I guess.

"Just go," Rika barked. "Go around him."

Damon swerved into the wrong lane, passing another car, and then jerked the wheel again, speeding on ahead, in front of it.

Taking out my phone again, I dialed Athos.

I should've called her right away. *Shit.*

"Hey," she giggled, and I could hear her friends' chatter in the background. "I'm not drinking. I might do some kissing. And I'm raising a little hell. Proud of me?"

"Go to the theater," I blurted out. "Now. It's an emergency. Stay there until I come and get you."

There was silence, and I half-expected to be questioned, but she didn't fight.

I heard her swallow. "Okay," she replied quietly. "I'll text when I'm there."

"Love you," I said.

"Love you too."

We hung up, and I looked at Rika who was listening in, her shoulders relaxing when I nodded.

We didn't ever overreact, and Athos knew it. If I sounded worried, I had cause, and she needed to do what she was told.

Rika reached behind and picked up a jacket out of the third row, pulling it on, and then dug under the seat, pulling out a blade. She kept them in all of our cars and various spots in the house for immediate access.

But I put my hand on hers, stopping her.

She met my eyes, and I shook my head. *No. Not this time.*

Her eyes narrowed, confused. "You can't be serious," she whispered. "I'm always with you."

My heart ached, because I never wanted to do anything without her. She was the reason we were who we were. It had all started with her.

My eyes dropped to her stomach, our son starting to show himself more every day.

"I need you to be with him," I told her.

At all costs.

"But Octavia and Madden—"

"We'll get them."

Of course, she was needed. And always wanted.

I touched her face, tipping her chin up to me, and the look in her eyes took me back to that night when she was thirteen, yelling at me over the hood of my car. "I've waited too long to see you and me walking around in one person," I murmured.

We loved Athos and we were lucky, because I didn't give a shit about the mother who'd left her at the sitter's when she was seven and never came back, or the father she'd never known.

She was made for us.

But I was dying for another chance to be a dad.

Damon swung into the parking lot of the marina, cliffs on both sides and snow pouring white over the sea. Rika finally nodded, knowing this was as far as she went.

"I'll call Search and Rescue." She took my phone out of my hand. "And direct the police when they get here."

I took her face and leaned in, kissing her as Damon and Winter jumped out of the car, and headlights fell upon us from behind.

71

Kai and Will were here.

"Lock the doors," I whispered against her mouth.

"Go." She kissed me again, her cheeks wet with tears. "Hurry. Bring them back."

I jumped out of the car, icy flakes hitting my face as I blinked against the snowfall.

"Let's go!" Kai shouted.

I ran, glancing once more at Rika through the windshield, but she was already on the phone as she leaned over the front seats, hitting the locks.

We raced down the steps and onto the dock, looking for any sign of movement or life among the boats, or out at sea.

"Jesus, it's getting bad," Emmy said, pulling Will's coat around her as she blinked against the downpour.

The black ocean loomed beyond, the darkness swallowing up any light. God, there was nothing. No kick up in the wake of a boat. No lights. Where were they?

I grabbed for my phone, but my pocket was empty. I forgot Rika had it. We needed more eyes on the town. I didn't know where Kai got his information, but they could be anywhere but here.

"Mr. Mori!" someone called.

We all spun around, and my eyes finally caught sight of the old man up on the second-floor balcony of the marina office.

Doones was about sixty-five and the last old sea dog Thunder Bay could brag about from back in the day, when we prided ourselves on our clam chowder, rather than our cheese and wine tastings.

Kai rushed up, shouting, "Did you see Octavia and Madden tonight? Which way did they go?"

"I didn't see anything," he called out, steam billowing from his mouth as stringy gray hair curled out from under his winter cap. "It's a winter storm comin'!" He held out his hand, announcing it as if we were all blind. "Just a few lads earlier came in from Pithom on a speedboat."

I shot forward a step. "What?" Pithom? They came in from my yacht? "Pithom is docked in the Keys for the winter. It's not here!"

"No, it's floatin' about a mile out," he informed me, "but..."

He leaned side to side as if searching behind us.

"Well, their speedboat is gone now, so they musta showed back up and returned to it."

And he didn't see when they'd returned. Which meant the kids could've been with them.

I jerked my eyes to Damon. "You got the key?"

He dug in his pants pocket and pulled out his key ring, the silver one with the black grip immediately visible. He'd taken the company speedboat out last week, trying to get a drone over Deadlow Island, but that was just between us. Rika and Kai would have our asses if they knew we were spying on the Moreaus.

"Go!" Damon ordered all of us.

We all ran down the dock, the red racing boat floating in its usual spot, and Doones shouting behind us.

"Sir, no!" he cried. "The visibility is getting worse by the minute. We can call the Coast Guard."

"No time!" Kai bellowed.

"Fuck," Damon bit out.

"East, by southeast," Doones called out, "judging from where they came when they arrived a few hours ago!"

Kai waved his thanks back at him.

"I swear, Kai," Will growled. "You tell that kid to light a fucking candle from now on."

"Shut up," Kai told him.

Everyone loaded onto the boat, Em, Winter, and Banks packed on the rear bench as Kai fired up the engine. Damon sat next to him, and Will stood in the middle.

I put one foot onto the craft but stopped. Glancing back over my shoulder, I saw the SUVs in the parking lot, Rika hidden behind the tinted windows.

It only took a moment, but I rolled my eyes and sighed. "Wait," I gritted out.

I couldn't leave her.

Charging back up the dock, I leapt up the steps, the cold air cutting through my lungs.

"Michael!" Kai hollered.

I heard the lock on the door click a moment before I yanked the handle, opening it.

Rika pinched her eyebrows together, gaping at me.

But I didn't have time to explain. Grabbing her hand, I pulled her out of the car, both of us breaking into as fast of a run as we could manage in her heels. I didn't want her to fall, and definitely not for the next few months.

We raced down the dock, and I pulled her on board, pushing her down into a seat and tightening my jacket over the one she already had on.

"You stay seated," I told her.

She nodded.

"Go, go!" Damon yelled at Kai.

Kai punched the gas, the propellers kicking up water behind us, and I grabbed on to the back of Damon's chair, holding on as we zoomed out of the harbor.

The frigid wind hit my hair, freezing my mouth, but I zoned in ahead of us, looking for any sign of the kids or the other boat.

How did they get Pithom? Why?

They must've been planning to hide them at sea

indefinitely. Why else would they have needed such a large vessel?

The wind sliced my skin as thoughts swirled in my head.

Ilia had been on Pithom, several times over the course of his employment with Damon's father, and Gabriel had been on the yacht many times with mine.

He would've known the boat. Would've known enough about us to probably gain access to it.

I knew I should've sold the motherfucker. Too much shit had happened on it, but instead of getting rid of it, I'd sent it south for the season to be refitted.

Goddammit.

"What the hell happened at the house?" I heard Emmy ask. "And in the car? His eye was torn out?"

I turned my head. "Whose eye?"

But it was Banks who answered. "The car we saw on the camera. It was crashed back near Old Pointe. Dinescu was in bad shape," she added.

"But then that just leaves Ilia," Will shouted over the wind. "He wouldn't be able to carry Tavi *and* Mads."

"If he had Octavia, Mads would just follow," Kai told us.

I glanced at Rika as she and Banks held Winter's hands.

"Just find them," Winter pleaded, her face etched with pain as tears filled her eyes. "Please, just find them."

She always tried to hide it, but I could only imagine how helpless she felt.

I spun around and dropped to a knee in front of her. "Stop it," I said, touching her hand. "Octavia needs to see you not scared."

The boat bounced over the water, my own eyes watering from the rush of wind.

"If it were Athos," she told me, "you'd be terrified."

I glanced at Rika again, a look passing between us.

"When it *is* Athos, you *will* be terrified," Winter said.

As if it was only a matter of time.

I clenched my jaw, not needing any explanation on what her point was.

She was right. We'd sent the kids to the dojo because we wanted to prepare them, but we were so arrogant that we never actually thought anyone would have enough balls to try anything.

"Our life creates enemies," she stated in a low voice.

Rika's eyes flashed to mine, and where I usually saw strength and reassurance, I saw uncertainty. We'd never stopped getting into shit, but our kids in danger from an outside threat hadn't happened before.

It would happen again.

What were we supposed to do? Hide? Be invisible? Live quietly?

Cower?

I didn't know how to be anyone else.

"Pithom!" I heard Will shout.

I rose to my feet, whipping around.

"Just barely," he added. "It's hard to make out in the storm."

I stepped up behind him, gripping his shoulder for support, and peered over the windshield, seeing the distant purple glow of the lights.

Damon rose from his seat, getting ready. "Thank God."

"Wait, what is that?" Banks called out.

I jerked my head, following her gaze.

Leaning closer to the edge, I clutched the side of the boat, barely able to make out something in the water.

"There's something there!" I shouted to Kai, pointing. "Over there!"

Kai turned the boat, and we grew closer, the small vessel

coming into view. Black hair and a black suit became clearer and clearer, and Banks cried out, "Mads!"

"Oh, my God." Winter's knuckles went white as she gripped Rika's hand and sat up straight. "Are they okay? Are they hurt? Do you see Octavia?"

"Stop, stop, stop!" Damon urged.

I locked my gaze on the kid in the boat, looking for anything to tell if he was hurt, alive, still in danger...

But Kai was going too fast to stop on a dime. He circled the other speedboat again and again, slowing down and finally puttering up to the side.

The still boat sat in the water, rocking side to side in the wake of our craft, and I looked over, seeing Mads holding a small form to his side. Streaks of blood lined the side of his face.

Shit.

I didn't see Ilia Oblensky anywhere. My stomach swam and sank at the same time. My hands shook, desperate to get over there, because if we didn't get them in our arms, they could still be lost.

Before Will could tie us off, Damon jumped into the other boat and crashed to his knees, taking Octavia's shoulders.

But her arms stayed around Madden.

Banks grabbed her son, hugging him to her, but he didn't let go of Tavi. "Are you okay?" she cried. "Are you hurt?"

She tried to tip his face up and look at him, but he just pulled away gently. "It's not my blood," he said quietly.

"Octavia?" Winter called out.

Kai dove down and grabbed his son's face, the kid looking as calm as ever with an impatient purse of the lips.

Ilia Oblensky slumped up against the dash panel, looking like the life was draining out of him.

"Mads?" Kai looked up at his kid. "You okay? What happened? Whose blood is this?"

The eleven-year-old just stared at his parents, his lips twisted to the side like he was bored. Octavia huddled close to him, shivering.

Other than some red cheeks and nipped noses, they looked okay.

Kai pushed off the ground and turned his attention to Ilia, grabbing the guy's collar. "You son of a bitch," he growled. "You put your hands on my child."

But Ilia wheezed as he breathed, and Kai hesitated, letting his eyes fall down Ilia's form.

He released him and ripped open his jacket. Blood coated his black shirt, his blond hair sweaty and matted.

We all stilled.

Kai yanked open his shirt, and I spotted the small holes and the blood spilling out of them. The color was draining from Ilia's face as he started to fade out. He had minutes.

"His lungs are punctured," Kai said, turning to look at us. "What the hell happened?"

And then to Madden. "Mads? What happened?"

Kai knew what had happened. We all knew. And Mads wasn't going to answer what was already obvious.

"She's cold," was all he said.

"Octavia," Damon said, trying again to pull her away.

Finally, she looked up at him. "Daddy."

She reached for him, and he pulled her into his arms, hugging her tight. "You okay?" he asked. "Did they hurt you?"

She shook her head, her braids and all the jewelry she had in her hair glinting in the moonlight.

She reached over his shoulder, into the night. "Pithom," she said, pointing to the yacht that was fading more and more into the horizon.

The waves kicked up, splashing us with spray, and I blinked against the snow, seeing that the sea was starting to get choppy.

"We'll get it," he assured her.

"It's getting farther away," she whined.

He climbed back onto our boat with her and put her in her mother's lap. "Don't worry."

Emmy and Will climbed back on our vessel with Rika, and I sat down in the seat next to Ilia, firing up the engine again.

"Call an ambulance," I yelled over to my wife.

She nodded.

Not sure how much good it would do. I should just dump the motherfucker overboard right now.

But I wouldn't deny Kai or Damon that pleasure. If the doctors saved him, we'd discharge him to the twelfth floor as soon as he was ready.

Punctured lungs. An eye torn out of its socket. A dead body at St. Killian's. I looked back at Mads, Kai desperate to see his son scared or need him, but...

Kai just held his son's face, wiping off the blood and trying to make eye contact.

"We're okay," was all he said, though.

Kai just stared up at him, no doubt thankful the kids were safe, but still uneasy.

"Let's just get them back to town," Banks told her husband. "They're freezing."

"I'll follow," I told them.

Kai led Mads onto the other boat with Banks, and I let them peel out of here before I immediately followed.

Ilia's head hung, bobbing with the bounce of the boat, and despite the cold air rushing at me, sweat dampened my skin.

We'd found them.

And Winter's words came back, winding their way through my head.

Our life creates enemies.

We chose this. The kids didn't.

What were our options? Separate as a family? Stop building? Go our separate ways?

The kids were in danger, but the kids also wouldn't want that. They all adored each other.

We threatened others, but we didn't ask for this. Others' behavior might end up being our problem...but not our responsibility.

We deserved what we had, and I wasn't fucking teaching Athos—or my son—that they didn't deserve exactly what they wanted. The last thing I would teach my kids was to cower, hide, or run.

We docked the boats, the ambulance already waiting to load Ilia onto a gurney.

But I was pretty sure he was already dead.

Or would be soon enough.

Emmy talked to the police, and I wasn't sure what story she was feeding them, but they knew we weren't going anywhere. We'd be here if they had questions tomorrow.

"Can we still open presents?" Octavia chirped, her usual cheerful voice back.

"Yeah," Damon laughed, hugging her to him again.

He put her in the car, Mads and Winter climbing in after her, but Kai hung back, running his hand through his hair.

As usual, he worried about everything, and I knew what he was worried about.

I was worried too, but I knew what was going through his head was far bigger than the doubts in mine.

I headed over to him, Will and Damon joining us.

"Jesus Christ," Kai murmured, needing to clear his head before he got in the car.

"We don't know anything," I reminded him.

He always got worked up before he knew he had something to worry about.

"'That kid's crazy,'" he said.

I studied him. "What?"

"That's what Dinescu said when his eyeball was hanging out of his head." He stared straight ahead. "'That kid's crazy.' You think Madden killed that guy at the house too?"

Will and Damon remained silent, and I knew what everyone was thinking. It freaked us out, but were we upset he did it?

"I think he's the reason they failed tonight," I told Kai, keeping my voice low. "Don't do this. I don't give a damn what happened to those pieces of shit. And neither should you."

Kai shook his head. "Michael..."

"Our life makes enemies," I stated. "Our strength threatens people."

I looked around, making eye contact with all of them. For years, I didn't stop them from doing whatever they wanted, because I wanted them to embrace what they were, but I was not going to let Kai feel like he'd done something wrong, when the alternative was Mads doing nothing and those kids being lost to us forever.

"We're not changing," I told them.

Kai stepped up to me, almost glaring. "And in another ten years when another enemy, or the child of an enemy, creeps up to surprise us again?"

"They won't want to mess with your kid in ten years," Will joked.

"This isn't funny!" Kai growled, not caring who heard him. "My kid—"

"Didn't go looking for any of this!" I finished for him. "None of this is his fault. He did what any animal on this planet does when someone threatens its life."

Kai fell silent, and I didn't back down. I knew what he was worried about. I understood. What if a bully got on Mads's last nerve someday? What if he got into a fight and caused more harm than he bargained for?

What if everything he'd learned at the dojo and with his grandfather had turned him into something we couldn't control?

But none of that would happen.

Not really.

Mads was taught just as much about when to fight as he was taught how to fight. The only thing that unnerved me was how much more efficient he was at it than me.

"Now, let's go home and light the fucking tree and tuck our kids in," I told all of them. "With any luck, what happened tonight spreads like wildfire, and anyone with a beef will think twice about coming for us or our kids again."

"Hell yeah," Damon muttered.

He and Will headed off, climbing into the cars, while Kai and I stayed with our gazes locked.

"We're all watching him," I assured Kai. "We're all raising him."

Kai wasn't alone.

His jaw flexed.

"He could be a million miles away, living in hell right now," I pointed out. "He brought himself and that little girl home tonight."

We taught soldiers to kill people to save a nickel on a barrel of oil. Whatever Mads did or didn't do tonight, he'd had no choice.

Finally, Kai's eyes dropped, and his chest caved as he nodded.

Mads was safe. That was all that mattered.

We walked to the cars, climbing in.

82

"Did someone say presents?" I called out as I buckled my seatbelt.

Octavia gasped and then yelped, already forgetting the incident, her sights set on the promise of everything under the tree.

After picking up Athos and the rest of the kids, Will driving the busload back, we returned to St. Killian's to find the winner of the treasure hunt waiting and ready for their prize.

The kids were shuffled upstairs to get bathed and into their pajamas, while Rika and I pushed through, presenting the trust to Tucker Adams and his girlfriend, Amanda Leigh. While David stayed at the Pope with Taylor and Kai, Damon and Will smuggled the body out of the house to the waiting truck, so Lev could deliver it to the coroner.

We had so much shit to deal with tomorrow.

And to try to keep quiet.

A round of applause, a champagne toast from the remaining guests, and the house finally started to empty after about forty-five minutes.

The kids rounded the fifteen-foot tree, lighting more candles as only a few remained lit in the whole house, the wind outside howling through the nooks and crannies of the old church.

I stood back, watching the kids open presents—except for the one they saved for Christmas Day—playing with their toys, showing off their new gadgets, and throwing the books to the side that we tried to make sure was on every holiday list, just in case they ever took an interest.

Damon held a package wrapped in brown paper, looking at it almost nervously, like he wasn't sure he was ready to open it, while Octavia ran to the window bench, plopping down next to Madden. She colored with her new Crayola markers that her parents had refused to trust her with up until now, as Mads sketched with his new pencils and pad.

She kicked her legs back and forth.

I slipped my arms around Rika, hugging her close. "Kids bounce back, don't they?"

My God.

She laughed. "I think Octavia knew what the rest of us didn't."

"Which was?"

"She was never in any real danger."

I watched the kids, Mads probably drawing another bird, as his cousin tried to act just like him with her purple marker.

"Have they caught the boat?" Rika asked me.

"The weather's too bad." I kissed her head, my hand resting on her stomach. "They'll need to wait until morning."

I wondered if there was anyone on it, or if the three men had manned it all on their own.

For all I cared, I hoped they never found it. That boat was cursed.

"Has he talked about it?" Rika asked.

Who?

But then I realized, she was still eyeing Mads.

I sighed. "I doubt he will."

Kai might've freaked out, but I wasn't sure it registered with his son. Mads's sense of empathy wasn't like others.

At least that I'd seen.

I gazed out at the scene, gold and red paper scattered all over the floor, while flames flickered on the tree, the red ribbons hanging down and looking so beautiful against the snowfall still coming down outside.

Tomorrow there'd be food and sledding, and maybe some football in the snow, because if there was anything we knew now, it was that every moment with each other was exactly where we belonged.

Treats covered the dining table as a fire burned in the fireplace, and Emmy started a record. I smiled, tightening my hold on Rika and hoping we never had to go through again what we went through tonight.

And if we did, please let it be years from now. My heart still hadn't slowed.

Athos tried to catch a peek at Mads's drawing, but he just turned away as she ruffled the hair on his head. I watched her walk over and climb up onto the windowsill across the room, sipping her punch while she watched everyone.

My heart fluttered, and I almost choked on the words.

"I watched you watching us from that window so many years ago." I pointed to where Athos now sat, remembering that Devil's Night so long ago. "Trying to not feel you there, but needing you to stay."

She leaned her head against my body.

"We were right about here when I sent you in blindfolded," I pointed out.

"Pushed me, you mean."

I chuckled. I was such a dick.

I was still a dick, but she loved me anyway.

She clasped my arms, hugging me back. "I wanted to feel everything, as long as I could feel it with you," she told me. "All these years later, that hasn't changed."

Not even an inch.

The music played and the children laughed, most of them completely unaware of what had happened tonight, although Rika had filled Athos in.

We created our life here.

One life. One chance.

"No one stops us," she whispered. "No one owns us."

I held her tight. "And we're not changing."

EPILOGUE

Mads

I rubbed my ears, the friction filling my eardrums and making the noise of the party fade and seem farther away than it was. Over and over again, I drowned out the chatter, the dishes being cleared downstairs, the doors opening and closing....

I liked noise. Rain and birds and wind. I just didn't like other peoples' noise. It made the room feel small. Too small. I couldn't think.

After presents and treats, I'd slipped into the upstairs bathroom, closed the door, and stood there for a couple minutes—maybe more—rubbing my ears as I closed my eyes. I hated that I did it.

I hated that it helped.

I hated that I had to hide to do it.

Because I hated the way Ivar looked at me years ago when he caught me doing it.

I could read the room by now. I knew I was never going to be him, and I knew what parts of me to keep quiet.

Sitting on the edge of the tub and holding my head in my hands, I listened to my breathing in my ears, hearing my pulse, and eventually felt everything slow. My heart. My breathing.

My thoughts.

I drew in a deep breath and slowly exhaled, feeling the steadiness and calm return.

Finally, I rose from my seat and turned to face the mirror, straightening my hair on both sides, and pushing the quarter of an inch growth behind my ears. I'd have my dad take me for a trim tomorrow. We usually went every other Saturday, but I didn't want to wait.

Pumping some soap into my palm, I washed my hands again, dried them, and then brushed my fingers down my clean black suit and straightened my tie, the habit of feeling my clothes making me feel secure. Like armor.

I exited the bathroom and turned off the light, heading to the boys' room we all shared when we stayed over at St. Killian's.

But heels hit the floor behind me, and I heard my mom's voice. "I have pajamas."

I glanced over my shoulder, stopping and taking in her dress. I loved it when my mom dressed up. It was pretty.

"I'm okay," I told her.

She narrowed her eyes. "Don't you want to sleep in something more comfortable?"

"I am comfortable."

I'd showered when we'd returned and changed into a fresh suit.

I started walking again, but I heard her step toward me. "Mads, I—"

I jerked my head. "No, don't come," I told her, turning to face her. "I want to be alone."

"I want to sit with you tonight," she told me.

My stomach knotted. That was the last thing I needed. I knew she was just trying to do what she thought parents should do, or she assumed I needed something that I didn't know I needed—like a talk or a hug or something—but parents made everything worse. I didn't need help.

"I'm okay," I said again.

Her eyes crinkled with worry, and I knew no matter what I did or said, she'd worry anyway.

I gritted my teeth and forced my feet to move over to her, diving in for a quick hug—patting her back twice—because I knew it would make her feel better. "I'm okay," I repeated.

Turning around, I headed down the hall, exhaling when I rounded the corner and she hadn't called me back or followed me.

Veering to the right, toward the boys' room, I saw my uncle swing around the corner of the hallway ahead and stop, meeting my eyes.

I stopped too.

Something weird crossed his black eyes, like a mixture of amusement and interest, and I braced myself as he walked for me.

I liked my uncle Damon. He didn't try to talk to me all the time.

Usually.

I watched, my spine stiffening as he leaned down to get in my face, the stench of cigarettes filling my nostrils.

"I know what you did," he whispered, keeping the words between us.

I stared at him.

"If my child is ever in danger, don't hesitate to do it again," he told me. "Understand?"

I remained silent.

But I knew what he was talking about.

I didn't understand most people. They acted like most decisions in life were a choice. Was I not supposed to do anything when those men came tonight?

That was why I'd kept my mouth shut. My parents would've freaked out if they'd lost us, and they still would've freaked out if they'd known how I'd stopped it. They would've just confused me. I didn't know what they wanted.

But Uncle Damon wouldn't make me respond to a question he'd already faced the answer to.

And he didn't seem upset.

"You got any bad feelings about what happened tonight?" he asked me.

I dropped my eyes.

The lie would make my parents worry. The truth would make them worry more.

"Yeah, didn't think so." He smirked. "If you ever do, you come see me. Got it?"

It took a moment, but I nodded.

He dove in and left a peck on my cheek before rising again and continuing on his way.

I waited until he was around the corner before I dug out the handkerchief in my pocket and wiped his tobacco spit off my skin.

Stuffing the cloth back into my pants, I walked into the dark bedroom. Ivarsen and II were on the other side of the room in single beds, and Gunnar was in the bed next to mine, his covers down around his feet.

Dag and Fane were up in their nook in the attic, while the girls were next door.

But as I walked to my bed, I spotted a lump under the covers. I moved closer, seeing long, black hair fanned out across my pillow.

Octavia.

I stopped, smelling her from here. Her mom bought her her own shampoo that seemed to seep into everything she owned—and everything I owned when she was close.

I wasn't old enough to remember Jett being born, but when Octavia came, it was the first time I remembered a baby being around. Perfect and fragile and already loved by everyone, no matter who it would be when it grew up.

I was like that once too. Before people knew me.

I tightened my fists, seeing the bruise on her arm.

Everyone else forced me to come here or go there and to be a part of things. Octavia always left what she was doing or who she was with and came to me instead. It was nice.

She stirred, drawing in a breath and turning onto her back.

I pulled the pillow out from under her, her head plopping onto the bed as I set the pillow to the side. "You're in my bed."

I crashed down next to her and propped my head up on the pillow against the headboard.

Reaching into my breast pocket, I pulled out a couple of squares of sketch paper and started folding.

She nestled close, tucking her head on my arm.

"Are you scared?" I asked her, not looking away from my origami.

"I was a little before." Her small voice, so tiny, made something hurt in my chest.

My hand slowed for a moment, and I swallowed. She was pulled away from me, taken out of the house, and out to the ocean in a snowstorm tonight.

But maybe it wasn't them who scared her.

She saw everything.

Everything.

"Why were you scared?" I asked, but I didn't breathe as I waited for the answer.

She shifted, looking up at me. "Weren't you?"

I said nothing, simply continued folding the dove as her warmth filtered through the arm of my jacket.

A little.

I cleared my throat. "Don't be afraid. It'll never happen again."

"How do you know?"

I finished the bird, holding it up against the shadow of the snowfall on the ceiling.

"Because next time, I'll be bigger," I said.

Turning to her, I set the bird under her chin, seeing her smile peek out, and pulled the covers up, tucking her in.

"They'll find Pithom," I told her. "Don't worry."

She nuzzled in again, closing her eyes. "They won't find it."

"Why not?"

"It's what I wished for on the bay leaf," she explained. "A ghost ship."

A ghost ship. I kept my mouth shut, not wanting to burst her bubble.

Pithom was a yacht with a tracking system. It wouldn't stay lost for long.

"I'm going to find it someday," she declared.

Yeah, okay.

I gazed down at her, her black lashes draping over her pale skin, and I almost wished it could happen for her. Her imagination was full of wonderous things, and I didn't have any imagination at all. I didn't want her to be like me.

The adventures in her head sounded like a different world.

I lifted my hand to move away the lock of hair on her cheek, but I stopped, putting my arm back down.

I forced down the lump in my throat as I stared at her. "Can I come?" I whispered.

"There's nothing you love at sea, landlubber," she teased with her eyes still closed. "No birds."

I turned away. *There are some birds.*

I didn't ever really want to go anywhere or see the world. I liked being home, anywhere I didn't have to face people or meet new people.

But if she was going...

"Can I come?" I asked again.

She nodded, yawning. "Mm-hmm. But I'm captain."

I bit back my smile, watching her drift off to sleep.

Ship or no ship, she was the captain of everybody, and she knew it.

Standing up, I pulled the covers tighter over her, tucking them under the mattress to keep them in place.

Rising up, I looked down at Octavia, the origami dove still tucked under her chin. The purple bruise on her arm from one of the men's hands stood out, dark and visible, even in the dim moonlight coming through the window.

I flexed my jaw, tightening my tie and smoothing back my hair again.

Do you have any bad feelings about tonight? he'd asked.

I had bad feelings all the time. When music was too loud. When my mother's dogs got hair on my bed. When Marina made a dish differently that I relied on her always making it the way I liked.

I watched Octavia sleep.

I had bad feelings when things were taken away from me.

Not about other things.

I brought up my hand, inspecting the dirt under my nail.

Using my thumb, I picked it out, noticing it was red.

I exhaled, my heart thumping in my chest.

Taking out my handkerchief, I wiped off my hand and walked to the window, reaching into my breast pocket and pulling out the bay leaf from earlier.

I hadn't burned it.

Slipping it between my lips and into my mouth, I chewed the leaf and swallowed it, the tickle down my throat reaching my stomach as the pungent taste coated my tongue.

I turned to sit in the chair, content to sleep there for the night and keep an eye out, but something glinted above me, and I looked up.

A key hung from the lock on the window, a small scroll of paper tucked in the chain.

I looked around the room, wondering who it belonged to.

Reaching up, I unhooked the chain from the lock, holding the skeleton key in my hand and pulling the paper out of the link.

Unrolling it, I read black handwriting. "The chords of the heart need to be touched to be played."

I narrowed my eyes, reading it again. I wasn't sure what it was telling me. Maybe it wasn't even meant for me.

I inspected the rusty old key and the keychain, what looked like a thurible hanging off the end.

I paused. Thuribles were used to spread incense at Mass. The cathedral in the village had a huge one.

My face fell. *That was a clue.* Thoughts and theories swarmed my brain.

I looked over my shoulder at Octavia, knowing how she would love an adventure. A hunt. This key went to something. Maybe a treasure?

"The chords of the heart need to be touched to be played," I recited again, trying to figure out what it meant.

Then it hit me. *No one is immune to emotion when those chords are pulled.*

No one.

I closed my eyes, feeling the blood under my nails as I wrapped my cold fingers around the key.

One night soon.

While everyone was asleep.

We'll find out what the key unlocks, Octavia. We'll own the night.

THE END

Thank you for reading *Fire Night!* I hope you enjoyed seeing the crew celebrate something other than Devil's Night, and I hope you have a wonderful holiday season.

Next up, we have *Tryst Six Venom, Motel,* and the kick-off to the Hellbent series. And maybe a couple little surprises, too. Get ready for 2021!

Acknowledgements

To the readers—I want to thank you so much for all the help and support over the years. I hope you enjoyed this treat, and although I don't have any ideas for more full-length novels in this world quite yet, it's always possible down the road. Send some good vibes to my brain (maybe lighting a candle or chanting will help, too) ;)

Until then, we have the Hellbent series coming, a lot of stand-alones, and I'm sure we'll see the Thunder Bay crew in more bonus content here and there for fun.

To my family—I could not have done nearly as much as I did this year without my husband. Thank you for being there, rolling with the homeschooling, and helping with things, so I wouldn't have to worry. Thank you to my daughter, as well! When Mom's office is at home, it's hard for kids to think of us as being "unavailable" like we would be at a regular job, so thank you for working on your problem solving and allowing me as much time as possible to work.

To Dystel, Goderich & Bourret LLC—thank you for being so readily available and helping me grow every day. I couldn't be happier.

To the PenDragons—Gosh, I've missed you all. There were so many days, especially a month into quarantine that I was desperate to spend some time with you. I needed people, and I really appreciate that you're my guaranteed happy place. Thanks for giving me a tribe and validating the stories I love.

To Adrienne Ambrose, Tabitha Russell, Tiffany Rhyne, Kristi Grimes, Claudia Alfaro, and Lee Tenaglia—the amazing Facebook group admins! Not enough can be said about the time and energy you give freely to make a community for the readers and me. You're selfless, amazing, patient, and needed. Thank you.

To Vibeke Courtney—my indie editor who goes over every move I make with a fine-toothed comb. Thank you for teaching me how to write and laying it down straight.

To all the wonderful readers, especially on Instagram, who make art for the books and keep us all excited, motivated, and inspired...thank you for everything! I love your vision, and I apologize if I miss things while I'm offline.

To all of the bloggers and bookstagrammers—there are too many to name, but I know who you are. I see the posts and the tags, and all the hard work you do. You spend your free time reading, reviewing, and promoting, and you do it for free. You are the life's blood of the book world, and who knows what we would do without you. Thank you for your tireless efforts. You do it out of passion, which makes it all the more incredible.

To every author and aspiring author—thank you for the stories you've shared, many of which have made me a happy reader in search of a wonderful escape and a better writer, trying to live up to your standards. Write and create, and don't ever stop. Your voice is important, and as long as it comes from your heart, it is right and good.

ABOUT THE AUTHOR

Penelope Douglas is a *New York Times, USA Today,* and *Wall Street Journal* bestselling author. Her books have been translated into fifteen languages and include *The Fall Away Series, The Devil's Night Series,* and the standalones, *Misconduct, Punk 57, Birthday Girl, and Credence.* Please look for *The Hellbent Series (Fall Away Spin-Off)* beginning in 2021 and the stand-alones, *Tryst Six Venom and Motel,* coming soon!

Subscribe to her blog
https://pendouglas.com/subscribe/

Follow to be alerted of her next release:
http://amzn.to/1hNTuZV
Or text DOUGLAS to 474747
to be alerted when a new book is live!

Follow on social media!

Spotify: https://open.spotify.com/user/pendouglas
Instagram: https://www.instagram.com/penelope.douglas/
BookBub: https://www.bookbub.com/profile/
penelope-douglas
Facebook: https://www.facebook.com/
PenelopeDouglasAuthor
Twitter: https://www.twitter.com/PenDouglas
Goodreads: http://bit.ly/1xvDwau
Website: https://pendouglas.com/
Email: penelopedouglasauthor@hotmail.com

And all of her stories have Pinterest boards!
https://www.pinterest.com/penelopedouglas/

Made in the USA
Las Vegas, NV
25 May 2023

72543251R00069